ELENA SOBOL

EMERGENCY DRAGONS

Copyright © 2023 by Elena Sobol

All rights reserved.

No portion of this book may be reproduced in any form without written permission from the publisher or author, except as permitted by U.S. copyright law.

Edit: www.copybykath.com

Cover Art: https://coversbychristian.com/

1

After six years of dragging idiots out of Hell, I'm used to humans being mad at me. What I am not used to is someone waving a high-heel shoe in my face. To be fair, the sparkly thousand-dollar stiletto probably qualified as a weapon under the Nevada state law.

"My daddy will hear of this!" the Barbie lookalike shrieked. Her sequin top was as muddy as her footwear. That's what happens when you get kidnapped and taken to the swamps of Nav. I ignored Rudy's smirk. Standing in the front lobby of the Spiral's posh reception area, he hadn't even bothered to defend me from the over-privileged wrath of the girl we rescued. Jerk. "You will get fired!" Her grin looked extra manic under the mascara smears. "I will see that you go down together with this whole 'agency'," she air quoted, "that thinks it's okay to ruin my dreams!"

I fought hard not to roll my eyes. The agency in question was the inter-dimensional police that was far scarier than her daddy. Or the creep that took her, for that matter. It had also taken us hours of trekking through sole-sucking mud to get her out, and it was only thanks to the ERS van's inter-pantheon traveling powers we weren't there still. With fatigue throbbing through my bones, I had to dig deep to find professionalism. Really deep.

I raised my hands in a placating gesture.

"Ma'am, you were taken from a nightclub by a foreign pantheon entity. You're very lucky that we found you in time." I spoke slowly, like I was talking to a child. "I don't think you understand what happened—"

"Don't you 'Ma'am' me!" she howled. "Gregory said he loved me! We were going to get married in Ibiza!" the girl howled. The stiletto dropped from her hand and she pressed her hands to her eyes. "He was so... so gorgeous. And now he's gooooone. It's all your faaauuult!"

Proceeding to sob in dramatic, practiced slurps, she eyed Rudy's tall frame through her fingers. I shook my head. If I was a supernatural spook looking for easy pickings in Reno, I'd go for this one, too.

Out of the corner of my eye, I saw Seline, the undine receptionist, press a panicked sequence of buttons on her phone. Despite the drama, I was relieved. Jennie was acting like she'd been kidnapped by Henry Cavill, but we were lucky to find her in one piece. When pretty girls disappear, it's usually for terrible reasons.

The elevator doors slid open behind us and Heal Hands swarmed us. Stepping aside, I let the medical crew handle our 'victim.'

"It's weird, isn't it?" I said to Rudy. "Why would she get taken to Nav, and then just left to wander around? And who is this 'Gregory'?

The reaper raised a sculpted eyebrow. After trudging through the bog, my partner didn't look any worse for wear. Instead of a rat's nest, his blond hair looked artfully tousled. Even the scrapes on his cheeks from our tangle with some reeds didn't ruin his good looks. He shrugged. "Perhaps a better question would be what Stonefield was thinking, sending us down there immediately after our trek through Duat. I'd barely had time to wipe the snake venom off my weapons."

He didn't have to remind me. My ankle still throbbed from one of the fangy bastards biting through my jeans. "You mean before or after we write a three-hour report?"

The reaper gave me a rare, wicked smile. "That's all you, partner. I have to call my superiors in Purgatory."

I groaned and rubbed my temple. "See you at the van?"

He nodded. "Don't be short with Director Stonefield," he warned. "Otherwise, he'll send us on another mission after lunch."

"Don't even say it," I said to him. "Mitten's forgetting my face as we speak."

With Stonefield being our new boss, we had no shortage of rescues that were barely punctuated by a bathroom break. Seeing how I'd turned my old boss into a pile of ash, I had no one to blame but myself. At least my neck-breaking schedule kept me from thinking about Zan. After he'd come back from his father's realm two weeks ago, he'd been weird. Distant. I didn't want to admit that it scraped my heart.

Another shriek rang through the lobby as the Heal Hands attempted to examine Jennie. Drawing a graceful arch, the high heel stabbed one of them on the shoulder. A pained cry came from the healer, and I winced.

Hell really hath no fury like a woman scorned. I would know.

Finally, someone had the smart idea of blowing a handful of pixie dust into her face. She sank onto the propped stretcher. The selkie siblings—Henry and Anne—positioned and strapped her down with long-practiced competence. As they wheeled her away, one of their coworkers took her purse and the stiletto to the receptionist. Presumably, to be turned over into evidence as weapons of assault.

The golden ammonite, the symbol of the Spiral, seemed to sneer at me from its perch over the reception desk. Reflecting the light of a faulty neon lamp in the lobby, it looked like it had a crack in its shell. You and me both, buddy.

Dragging my fingers through my tangled hair, I pulled it up into a bun. My ankle throbbed, my muscles ached, and I would really feel that swamp trek in the morning. As the Heal Hands disappeared into the elevator, I resigned myself to grabbing the paperwork from the front desk. Reports don't write themselves.

"Hey, Chrys?" Seline's voice startled me as I turned to leave. After I'd killed Asmoday in Hell, she'd started actually acknowledging me when I came around. It never stopped being weird.

"Yeah?"

She reached into the pink Prada purse on her lap that I recognized as Jennie's. A golden envelope appeared in her green hand and the delicate gills on her neck flared.

"This is for you, I think." She sounded as confused as I felt as she handed it to me.

The smell of smoke and men's cologne wafted up at me. What the hell?

"What is it?" I asked, feeling too dumb from exhaustion to process this properly.

"I don't know, but it has your name on it." It sure did, written in a gorgeous script.

"To: Chrysoberyl Green, Veles' Daughter."

Shrugging, I put it under the stack of files. Maybe it was a practical joke, or a letter from a long-lost great uncle. At the moment, I didn't care. I had bigger problems waiting for me upstairs. One big problem, to be exact, and it was probably stuffed into an expensive suit and already smoking with fury.

The Spiral's building in Reno is situated in the City Hall. A mortal walking through the double doors of the modern high-rise wouldn't see the holograms on the walls or the golden elevators taking all manner of supernatural employees up and down the levels of the inter-pantheon law enforcement. Rudy and I were agents of the ERS—Emergency Rescue Services. We rescued souls in various Underworlds from Hades to Nav, my father's pantheon. It's not all heroics and grateful victims rescued from the brink of death. Mostly, it's sore muscles and mounds of paperwork for pissed off humans who had no idea what even happened.

Just ask Jennie.

After taking the elevator up, I walked past the row of offices to Stonefield's lair. Murmurs of greetings followed in my wake. Like Seline's friendliness, this was also new. Rudy and I had officially become heroes of the department three months ago, and I didn't think that it sat well with Stonefield. He'd been wrong when he accused me of eating souls that Asmoday had stolen. That sort of thing gets people talking. If he wasn't a fan of mine three months ago, he definitely wasn't one now.

I knocked on a wooden door. Unlike everything else in the building, it was made of beautiful old oak. A grunt answered my intrusion, and I pushed my shoulder against the wood.

"Director," I said. "You wanted me to give you a report?"

Dark bookcases lined the walls and were filled with meticulously collected tomes that were organized by size and color. Tastefully arranged antlers, skeletons and desiccated spiders were displayed with lights over them. Hourglasses filled the space. The delicate vessels dotted the shelves, the windowsill, even the massive desk of the big man himself.

Stonefield glared at me from his giant leather armchair that might as well have been a throne. His bald head reflected the chandelier above and his blue suit highlighted the golden sheen of his otherwise human-looking skin. He was a man of significant size—and appetite, if his belly was anything to go on. His muscled arms kept him from looking comical. The half-djinn bared his teeth, causing a trail of smoke to escape his lips.

"Sit," he said.

I did as I was told. The stack of files in my hands hit the table.

"Care to explain why I have a human oil tycoon crawling up my ass about his daughter?" he steepled his thick fingers. "I thought I told you this was a delicate matter."

"She wasn't herself, sir," I said. "We brought her back, but she appears addled. The Heal Hands will erase her memory."

His glower deepened. "You should've pacified her at the scene. Now, I have a crazed woman who demands that we compensate her for 'emotional distress' and a father whose influence allows him an unwelcome insight into the supernatural world."

"I couldn't knock her out," I said to him. "The van was stuck in the bog, and it would have taken—"

"It doesn't matter what it takes," he growled. "You follow the orders of your superiors." He gave me a good, long stare as I fought to control my temper. "Other Underworlds aren't Hell, Green—you have to use your brain. Once Hell is up and running, you better believe that you'll be back to stomping your boots in devourers' sand dunes."

I nodded. Rudy would wrinkle his nose, but I couldn't wait. Asmoday's army did some damage to the entrance to Lucifer's realm. There was a weird rot that Uncle Ophis—the universal plumber who powered our vans—was investigating now. Until he deemed the passage safe, there would be no ERS vans passing the Gates. I hadn't been to Hell in weeks.

"Fill these out," he slapped the stack I'd placed in front of him. "To my satisfaction."

"Yes, sir," I bit out.

I wasn't sure whether to groan or to cry as I got to work. Obviously, the reports weren't anything new. However, the Director was known to ask so many questions that I wanted to eat the pages just so I could choke on them and die.

"What is this disturbance that you're talking about?" he asked twenty minutes later as he peered under my hand. It was question number eleven in our joyous time together. I was counting.

I suppressed a sigh. "I've been to Nav many times as a teenager," I said. "And this time the air felt—weird."

"The air felt weird?" He scoffed.

"Yes." I got my breathing under control. Rudy owed me big time. "Usually, Nav smells like gold and kissel—the cranberry drink that runs through the pantheon instead of water—and this time it smelled... Well, dead. There was an absence of something."

That seemed to intrigue him. "Have you told Slayer Hrom about this?"

My chest tightened at his mention of Zan. He'd been gone to serve his father from April through the end of May. Since he returned, he'd barely spoken to me. The words he'd said to me in Hell were so fresh in my memory, I still tasted them like ash on my tongue. I hated myself for repeating them until my chest ached.

I'd go to war for you, Veles' daughter.

"I have not," I said to Stonefield.

"And your father?" he pressed.

I didn't know why he was making a big deal out of my casual observation, but I kept irritation out of my tone. Barely.

"Veles sleeps in the roots of the World Tree for a decade at a time," I said. "Last time I saw him was ten years ago. He won't emerge for another year."

My father was the dragon god of the Slavic pantheon, hence my ability to turn into a dragon. He was a god of cattle and magic, as well as the guardian of Nav. I barely knew the man.

Fatigue was turning into a migraine in my temples, and I fought the urge to lean my forehead against the stack of files and sleep.

"Can I go?" I asked. "Sir," I added.

Stonefield waved his hand impatiently.

I left his office and turned the corner toward the elevator. My boss and I went a while back. We hadn't liked each other since I was an ERS trainee, and I wasn't holding my breath that it would change anytime soon. Bed was calling my name, and I couldn't wait to snuggle with Mittens—my ghost kitty—and forget all about Jennie and Stonefield and especially, Zan.

My nose slammed into something solid before my addled brain made me stop going. A wide chest blocked my vision, and I looked up to see the gray eyes of a thunder demigod who was the person I least wanted to see after being scolded by Stonefield—Zandro Hrom.

2

Perun's son towered over me like a mountain of hotness. His sharp jaw was scruffy, and his hair was longer than the day I'd woken up to him making me breakfast. Visiting Eagle Nest, his home in the Nevada Sierras, seemed like a lifetime ago. He wore a white shirt that strained over his muscles and I could see dark tattoos standing out under the fabric. Monsters and demons roared up from his skin like they were living things. There was more black ink than skin under his clothes. His hair was pulled back into a loose bun that let strands escape and frame his face. In my exhausted state, the memories of his body crushing against mine and his lips searching my mouth were too much to handle. In the spring, he'd saved me from a succubus that almost got me for years of servitude. Then, out of everyone on the Spiral, he had believed me when I said that Chief Baran was Asmoday. He'd broken the Spiral's law to save me, and his care had been like a balm over a festering wound. Then, two weeks ago, he'd returned and had iced me as if what had happened between us was nothing. I wasn't sure how I felt about that, and I wasn't ready to get into it. If he wanted to be nothing, we'd be nothing.

I took a step back and thrust my chin up to him.

"Slayer Hrom," I said evenly.

He looked shell-shocked at the sight of me. There was a rise and fall of his chest.

"Hey, uh, Chrys," he said.

I pushed past him. "Right. Have a good day." He caught my forearm.

"Wait—"

My throat tightened, and I made myself swallow. Who cares if he'd saved me from certain death? Many people have. I wasn't exactly an indestructible tank, and I worked in a dangerous profession. He'd been gone for weeks, but he didn't owe me an explanation just because he saved my life. Or just because we'd dated as teenagers, and now... I drew in a deep breath through my nose.

"Pretty sure this isn't work-appropriate," I said as I looked at his tattooed fingers grasping my elbow. They scorched my skin, and I refused to look up at him. Who was I to demand answers? I should've been grateful he'd kept me alive and left it alone.

"Sorry, yes. Highly inappropriate," he said with a smile. "Better alert the HR."

I bit the inside of my cheek. "Let go."

He released me immediately, and we stood in the corridor in awkward silence. I wished my hair wasn't reeking of a swamp and I had been wearing something else besides mud-splattered jeans and my beat-up Docs. Scratch the Docs, actually. Love my babies.

"You know I care about you," he said. "I think I've made that pretty obvious."

I grit my teeth. Never mind, on not knowing how I felt. "Angry" was a pretty good descriptor.

"Yeah, that's why you've hardly said two words to me since you got back."

"Chrys," he said. He raked back loose strands from his forehead. The smell of rain made my head swim. "My duty to Vyraj, and to my father, is something I was born to. It's not like I want to keep things from you. Sometimes, I have to make choices I don't want to make."

Like keeping his distance, I filled in. Veles and Perun were mortal enemies and their rivalry had gone back centuries. This is why we broke up when we were teenagers. In the spring, circumstances and one hell of a nasty demon drew us back together. Now, we were back to snapping at each other in the hallways. I raised my chin up at him.

"You don't owe me an explanation," I said.

He gave me a frank look. "Don't I?"

I was quiet for a long moment. He waited.

Finally, I shrugged. "I just thought it was a bit rude of you to keep your coworkers worried."

"I had to—do certain things to stay on my father's good side," he said. His gaze was heavy on me then, and I knew what he hadn't said. He was in trouble with his father for saving me, the daughter of his enemy. Not to mention breaking the inter-pantheon treaty to do it.

Heat rose to my cheeks, but I looked him full in the face, anyway. My anger boiled over.

"You shouldn't care so much," I said. "You're a demigod, and you work for the Spiral. How much more duty do you need?"

He jerked his chin like I had slapped him. "You don't know what you're talking about," he ground out. "You grew up in the human world."

We glared at each other. "Gods don't care about us," I said. "They stay in their pantheons, and the only time they come out is to screw something up."

I wanted to press my hand to his chest and feel the heat of his skin under my palm. I wanted many things, but I wasn't delusional enough to actually hope for them.

"Vyraj needs me," he said.

I took a deep breath. "It doesn't matter—"

"It matters to me," he cut me off. His next words were softer. "I wish you would try to understand. When was the last time you even connected to Nav? After getting your powers?"

"I don't need to go there to know where I belong," I said.

"It doesn't hurt to be connected," he said. "Maybe you'd stop judging your *coworkers* if you just took a moment to get in touch with that other part of yourself."

My eyes found the floor as I stared down, refusing to look at him.

"See you around the water cooler," he said, and walked away.

I bit my tongue before a "fuck you" could escape my lips. I'd been spending entirely too much time texting with Tick. At least the demon spawn understood childish anger, and man, was I feeling a lot of it right now. Even if I couldn't really be mad at Zan, I wanted to be mad at something.

The universe obliged me on the way to the elevator. As I shifted my grip on the report folders, a golden envelope slipped from under the stack and fluttered to the ground. The letter from Jennie's purse. Tearing through the paper with my name on it, I glared at the white card within. An intricate gilded border framed it. I hadn't imagined it—the letter was cologned with a heavy hand, like someone had sent me a love note in 1865.

"Dearest Chrysoberyl," it read. "Please forgive the unorthodox method of my communication. The girl I'd taken was treated with utmost care, and I never intended to harm her."

Forget cleaning up my language. A series of swear words rolled off my tongue.

"As your father, Veles, slumbers, I have no choice but to call to the duty in your blood. Something was taken from the pantheon, and I require your assistance in finding it in the human realm. Call on me at your earliest convenience." A golden card slid into my palm. It pictured a three-headed dragon. There was an inscription, but no number and no name. Annoyance set my teeth on edge.

Duty in my blood? I couldn't think of a worse time for someone to hustle me for *duty*.

This wasn't the first time someone tried to recruit me since I killed Asmoday. This Nav creature—whoever he was—wasn't even the only pantheon member to try to get me to help with their "little problem". Apparently, you kill one demon prince and everyone thinks they can hire you as a supernatural hitman. The last hopeful was a troll who'd ambushed me on the way to work. He thought I'd be the perfect person to settle his dispute with a neighboring goblin, presumably by biting his head off in my dragon form. Well, that explained why Jennie was hanging around ankle-deep in the swamp, waiting for us to find her. Waiting for *me* to find her.

"The nuts on this guy," I said as I balled up the envelope in my fist. I kept the card. I had absolutely no intention of reaching out to him, of course, but the Legal department might be interested in this turn of events. Duty in my blood? My duty lay in protecting the humans from supernatural exploitation, and this asshole had the nerve to kidnap someone to get my attention. That was grounds for some serious dungeon time. I'd drag him there myself, just as soon as I scrubbed two layers of dirt off my skin and ran my uniform through three wash cycles. Clutching the stack of report papers, I jammed the elevator call button.

Rudy waited for me at the van. His back supported the barn doors and one of his long legs was bent at the knee, which made him look like a surly black flamingo. He was lean, and would've bordered on gangly if his body didn't have a natural reaper grace. Reapers weren't exactly human. Their souls were bound to Christian Yawei for a major trespass during their human life. To atone for their sins, they were stripped of their human memories and reborn in Purgatory. Rudy had been a reaper for a long time, and my partner for just over a year. The ERS rescuer job was his side hustle. Usually, I avoided thinking about what he did in his spare time. I did like being able to sleep through the night. In his human skin, he looked like a pretty blond guy in his mid-to-late twenties, but it did not fool me. His death magic was clear in the skull that gleamed under his skin. I was one of the few people that could see it and I think it was because my dragon consumed souls. Something inside of me sensed death magic. The surrounding air chilled as I walked closer to him.

"You look happy," he said. "Was Stonefield as unpleasant as he always is?"

"He's not unpleasant to you," I pointed out. "I'm the only one that gets the VIP treatment."

"Few people are unpleasant to me." He gave me a rare smile. "It's bad for their health."

I couldn't agree more. You didn't want to make an enemy of the literal personification of Death.

I handed him the card from my pocket. "Look at this pile of demon crap."

His eyebrows rose into his hairline as he scanned the letter. "Someone really doesn't care about keeping their head on their shoulders. I'm almost impressed."

He handed it back to me. "Any idea who this is?"

"If I did, we'd be making an unscheduled house call right now," I said. "I'll handle it later. How was your call home?"

His lips thinned at the mention of Purgatory. "I'm being summoned," he said.

"What, where?"

"Back home," he said. "Apparently, there has been a theft in one of the record keeping offices. I'm being called back to investigate."

"For how long?" I asked. I didn't cherish the idea of having to pair up with someone else, like, say, Astrid. The burly Valkyrie has been looking for an excuse to kill me for years.

His arms crossed, he shrugged. "Hard to tell. I will keep you informed of when I expect to return." At my expression, he added: "It's my pantheon, Chrys. I have to do what I have to do."

"So everyone keeps telling me," I muttered.

"I'll text you when they release me from duty," he said. "The signal is poor there, but its adjacent enough to the human world to have a little. I'll be at the University."

I nodded. I was a big girl and could handle Astrid for a few days.

"Maybe I'll take time off and go tan somewhere for a week," I said to Rudy. Not running into Zan for a while seemed like heaven, actually. "Seeing how I have, like, three months saved."

He gave out a short laugh. "Sure you will."

3

"DON'T YOU KNOW THIS already? I'd go to war for you, Veles' daughter."

Zan smiled at me through the purplish haze of the summer sky, and I reached for him. His scruff was soft under my fingers. The heat of the night made my skin prickle. Lightning cracked in his pupils and I gasped as I felt electricity shoot through me. His hands followed it as they made a slow path up my hips and onto the planes of my stomach. Following the curves of my belly, they traced my skin in slow, languorous circles. My breath quickened and my lips opened and all I wanted to do was taste every inch of him. His finger pressed my lower lip as his face filled my vision. Grabbing my hips, his hands yanked them forward as his mouth fell on my mine. My eyes fluttered shut—

His finger spouted tiny needles and dug into my lip. My eyes flew open, and I wasn't in the purple lust-filled dream anymore. Covered in sweat, I was tangled in my blankets and my asshole cat was staring at me from my pillow, paw in my mouth.

"Mittens!" I batted the little paw away.

His faintly glowing kitty mug managed to look imperial. Somehow, the saucy feline had inched me off my pillow and to the edge of the bed where my ass dangled dangerously close to falling off. Now, he was bored and woke me up in the most effective way known to all cats. I groaned and buried my face in the sheets. The combination of the relentless summer heat and my libido made the nights impossible to get through. My one-bedroom apartment overlooked the Truckee River, but not even the supposedly "cool" air from the water helped with the ancient air conditioner that squeaked and rattled through the vents. Nevada summers are its own beast.

I sat up and looked at the lightening sky. I'd got a few hours of sleep before Mittens had decided I'd rested enough. Pulling the ghostly little asshole onto my lap, I scratched him behind the ears. He was partially incorporeal, but I could still give him pets.

"I'm being stupid, huh? Pining for some guy in the middle of the night." His muzzle made it obvious what he thought of me thinking of anyone but him. I kissed him on top of his head, anyway. "I know, baby."

I checked my phone. There were only three texts from Stonefield that gave me a new assignment, which was an improvement from his usual twenty-five. It'd been a week since Rudy left, and I was stuck driving with random crew members. Maybe my boss was busy with torturing someone else. Who was I to deny the man his hobbies? I rubbed my face. There was a good reason Stonefield and I didn't like each other, and it had nothing to do with Asmoday.

I had been nineteen and full of piss and vinegar when I'd joined the ERS academy. Two years of grueling practice had seemed like forever then, but looking back, it had gone by in a season. After my friendless childhood, I had befriended the quiet kid in my class. Jeremy was a grandson of one of the princes of Demons. The other trainees took care to avoid him. From the moment I slapped my lunch tray on his table and told him to move over, he'd followed me around like a puppy. When we were ready to graduate, all of us stood side by side on graduation eve, ready for the first real run that would turn us from trainees into ERS operatives.

I was pumped and ready to go. My ERS uniform was brand new and my boots were shining with new polish. When Clementia walked into the room, Jeremy stared at her with slavish adoration. The Goddess of Mercy was tall, statuesque, and her hair fell to her shoulders in waves that were shinier than freshly polished gold. Her skin was alabaster, and her eyes so luminous they dimmed everything in sight as they swept around the room.

"After today, you will embark on the journey of Mercy. You will be heroes and rescuers and will forever change the world with your compassion. I am proud of each one of you."

My lungs swelled with pride at her praise. Her beautiful, pure voice made me want to hear her praise repeatedly. She made me feel special, like I could erase my grave mistake and balance the scales. I nudged Jeremy, and he blinked at me like he was coming out of a daze.

We exchanged goofy grins and shared a bench in the van that took us down to our very first Underworld.

Duat greeted us with the humid smell of the River of the Night. We were let out in the 4th hour, trapped in a labyrinth of snakes where we were trained. It was a desert region—no matter what I did, my water-loving ass couldn't get away from the desert—and a straight up labyrinth. Hidden doors contained more and more of those damned winged snakes that came up to our hips and sank their fangs into us. Their feathery wings were sharp as razors and all twenty of us were bloodied and limping by the time we passed through the false doors. The only person who didn't go through was Jeremy. Earlier, I recalled him doing something he wasn't supposed to. Now, my gaze was impatiently trained on the last trick door I'd just stumbled out of.

"Come on," Astrid had pulled on my sleeve. Back then, she'd worn her pale hair cropped close to her head. Even then, she was shiny and proud, like a silver trophy.

"You can't just stand here."

I looked back at her, unsure. "He can't be much longer. I can wait."

"We'll be late to our graduation ceremony," she insisted. "He's a clever little weasel. He'll be fine."

Clementia laid a hand on my shoulder. "He will be alright, child. His fate is in the hands of the gods now."

I looked up into her eyes that moved with stars and the wisdom and compassion of the universe. She seemed to carry the absolute truth of all things. I nodded and followed her out. Jeremy would be okay; I was sure of it.

"Yes, ma'am."

The graduating party came and went with all of us freshly showered, salved and wearing our newly minted ERS uniforms that replaced our trainee garbs. Jeremy still wasn't there. When the lights came on, my nerves were frayed and I was so raked with anxiety that not even the two shots of tequila the other graduates poured into me were helping my nerves.

Clementia was sitting on her chair, surrounded by the heads of the Spiral that were sitting there kissing her ass. I remember the worshipping look on Stonefield's face as he poured the goddess a goblet full of wine that looked ridiculously expensive.

"Where is he?" I asked when I approached her. No "ma'am" for her this time.

She looked at me blankly, and Stonefield's small eyes burrowed into me in outrage. How dare I use that tone with a goddess older than the Spiral itself?

Her luminous eyes looked at me in mild confusion. Her beautiful mouth drew an 'O.' "Who are you talking about, young one?" she asked.

"Jeremy," I ground out through my teeth. "You promised you would get him out of Duat."

Clementia looked bewildered over the rim of her glowing goblet. Everything around her seemed to radiate just from being around her perfection. I hated it.

"I said no such thing, young one," she said. "Young Jeremy broke the law of the divine. He's in the hands of the gods of Duat and they will do what needs to be done. What is proper."

"He wanted to be a rescuer," I said. "This is his life's dream."

"Gods provide a proper place for every creature, human, and demigod in this world."

"You're a goddess of mercy," I said. "Where is your mercy?" I knew I was out of line, and I didn't care. "He worshiped you."

"As well he should, young Chrys," Clementia's voice was soft, magnanimous. Understanding. "There is an order to the universe. You performed admirably today. You are Veles' daughter, yes?" Her eyes softened, and I wanted to punch them. "Know your place in the order of things, and you will fulfill your purpose."

"Save him," I pressed.

She spread out her arms. "There's nothing to save. He's been dealt with according to the will of Egyptian gods."

"I—"

A burning hand fell on my shoulder. I looked up to see Stonefield digging his fingers into my shoulder. His arm was literally on fire.

"Forgive her, your holiness," he said to Clementia. "She's young and had too much to drink. Her rudeness is on my head."

The goddess inclined her head and turned back to her goblet and ass-kissing worshipers. I was dismissed and Jeremy's disappearance with me.

Stonefield marched me away from her table and turned his full djinn wrath on me.

What the hell is wrong with you, agent?" he hissed. "You're embarrassing your class."

I gestured at Clementia. "She threw him under the bus! He was one of our own."

A muscle twitched in his face. He knew I was right, but he wasn't willing to throw his career away for it. In that moment, I hated him for it, and he hated me for knowing that deep down, he we would put the department's reputation over its people.

Fast forward six years, and here we were. Squabbling over missions. You'd think that he would've moved me to work under someone else but maybe the man was as much of a glutton for punishment as I was.

Swinging my legs out of bed, I checked the time on my phone. Four a.m. If there was a point in going back to bed, I didn't see it. I searched the clean laundry basket for the least wrinkly pair of jeans and squeezed into them. Time for a Red Bull and a two-day-old donut. Breakfast of champions.

A knocking came from my balcony. My hands grabbed my gun and my horns pierced the top of my head. My mind reeled as I reached my dragon senses through the window screen outside to see if there was a soul. A human, my dragon told me. Kind of. Some sort of demon spawn burglar? Wouldn't be the first time one knocked me upside the head in my apartment. Then why would they knock?

Sliding off the bed, I made as little noise as possible as my bare feet crossed the floor. I pushed the balcony screen door shut, and I fell to the side of it, back against the glass. Breathing in and out of my nose, my toes pushed against the handle. In two moves that would make Rudy proud, I slid the screen open and leapt outside.

The figure standing there was just out of reach of the light streaming from my neighbors' windows. It was massive, at least six-and-a-half feet tall. Judging by his size, it could've been a werewolf or a goddamn Winnebago. The barrel of my gun found its head.

"Freeze, douche," I said. "Unless you want a new hole in your face." My gun was loaded with salt shavings, but it wouldn't hurt to exaggerate a bit on the off-chance my "guest" was human. The figure shifted and turned toward me. Suddenly, despite the blistering summer heat, I could taste rain on the tip of my tongue. Rain? My gun shook in my hand.

"Hey Chrys," Zan said. "Sorry to just drop in."

He stepped into the light, and I saw he was only wearing his jeans. Monster tattoos grinned, howled, and roared from his bare chest. Real and not real. His hair was loose and slightly curling around his shoulders. My breath stopped somewhere in my solar plexus at the sight of him. Then, the anger I felt about his silence returned. My jaw hardened, and I kept my gun trained on him. This was honestly too much, and I fought the urge to pinch myself to see if this was an extension of my embarrassingly naughty dreams about the thunder demigod.

A smile tugged his lips. "You can't kill me with salt rounds."

"No," I agreed, "but it would burn like a mother, and it's no less than you deserve for scaring the shit out of me."

Without a shirt to hide them, I could see the hollow shadows in the divots of his torso—a smear of black between his clavicles and under his chin. A much trimmer waist accompanied them. He looked like he'd spend a week in a hard labor camp.

He looked at my horns, specifically at the one that was rounded at the tip. "It's growing back," he said. When rescuing me from Lafayette, he'd accidentally dropped me in eagle form and I broke my horn on a rock. I wasn't too fond of thinking about that night. Mostly.

"No thanks to you," I said. "What happened to staying away from me? Your moods are giving me a whiplash, Hrom."

"I didn't come here to fight," he said. He looked tired and in critical need of a sandwich. "Chrys," taking a deep breath like the next words would hurt him, he said, "I need your help."

4

My gun lowered, and I frowned up at him. "Help with what?"

His jaw hardened. "There's something weird going in Vyraj. The pantheon is becoming unstable, and the creatures are scared."

"Unstable?" I asked. "Unstable how?"

He crossed his arms across his chest. "Earthquakes and fires, as well as cracks in the earth." He shook his head. "My brothers and I are investigating, but it's too chaotic. My father is gathering Vyraj's magic workers and demigods to help repair the damage, but it's not working very well."

I stared at him. Vyraj was technically the second layer of reality of the Slavic pantheon. Sandwiched between Nav and Prav—Perun's layer of reality—it kept the two separated.

"Cracks in the earth," I echoed. "Is the disturbance coming from Nav?"

He jerked his chin. "It seems like it, but it's hard to tell. Just because it's coming from below doesn't mean it has something to do with it. However—"

"What?" I asked.

"There are rumors," he admitted. "That a stabilizing artifact has gone missing from Nav, and that's what's causing the disturbance."

I swallowed and slid my gun back into its holster.

"Can I trust you with the refugees?" he asked.

This was so not what I was expecting. "What refugees?"

"We evacuated creatures from Vyraj, but the Eagle Nest is running out of space," he said. "I need more space for them. A safe space."

"And my tiny apartment came to mind?" I asked.

"You're a creature of Vyraj," he said. "You speak Old Slav."

I had to laugh at that. "Barely."

He smiled. "You smell like home," he said. "They will trust you."

I raised an eyebrow at him. "That is a very weird thing to say."

His expression unreadable, he leaned closer to me. This close, I could see tiny sparks of lightning in his irises and was suddenly too hot in my tank top and jeans.

"I know they'll be safe in your place," he said. "We will stabilize Vyraj and come back for them."

"But—"

"Please, Chrys," he said. "You want nothing to do with our pantheon, and that's okay. More than okay. You're a rescuer and there are people who need you here. I know we haven't seen eye to eye, but help me with this. They need a place to go while I take care of this mess."

Feathers grew out of his shoulders and I knew that our time was up.

"Wait," I said. "Something doesn't seem right. This sounds dangerous."

He stiffened and looked over his shoulder, like he was expecting for someone to be peering back at him from the dark. "I have to go."

A million questions erupted in my head, but I made myself ask what I hoped was the correct one.

"What's this artifact, Zan?"

The tawny eagle feathers were now covering his chest, and his eyes were yellow. "From what I hear, it's lost between the pantheons."

"What's it called?" I pressed.

He leaned onto the balcony rail and wings burst out of his shoulders, replacing his arms. It was beautiful and terrifying. Once, I'd ridden on his back, and now I'd give my left foot to have him carry us both away to Hawaii or something. I gasped as he leapt down and disappeared into the darkness.

"Fern Flower," the wind carried to me.

In my kitchen, I decided it was pointless to go back to sleep. I pulled out a Red Bull instead and popped the tab. It was the right decision because as soon as the sour bubbles hit my tongue, there was a knock on my door.

Those must've been the refugees Zan was talking about.

Dispelling the wards overhead, I pulled on the handle.

A familiar tiny face covered in soot stared up at me. The creature was wearing a grimy apron and her hair was pulled up into a messy topknot. She carried a bindle stick over her shoulder. I recognized her instantly.

"Bava," I stared down at the kikimora that ran the Eagle Nest, "what are you doing here?" I couldn't imagine Zan kicking her out to move in another creature.

She sniffed. "Master Zan bid us to come here. He said it would be safe."

"Who is 'we'?" I asked. "You're by yourself."

Her large yellow eyes returned to stare up at me. "My cousins are here with me. We are grateful for your hospitality." She peered around me and at the absolute mess that was my beloved apartment.

"But—" I started.

She gave a low, sharp whistle, and I stepped back in surprise.

Humanoid creatures suddenly filled the entire floor beyond my apartment. They rose just to my knee. Unkempt beards, aprons, and round, owlish eyes stared up at me in clear apprehension. They carried various knapsacks, bindles, and baskets full of their belongings. There looked to be no end to them as they filled the grimy carpet that stretched left and right to the doors of my neighbors. They were domovois, the house spirits of Vyraj.

"Oh," I croaked. "Hi."

Bava looked at me, and my heart sank at the pleading in her eyes. She sniffed again, and her eyes flicked back at her horde, as if she was unsure of their welcome. Just from a quick headcount, there were at least fifty of them.

How were they all supposed to fit in?

"They've lost their homes," she said. "Master Zan promised to stop the big destruction and return..."

Domovois were bound to their homes and hardly left them. Usually, several generations lived in the same house. To lose that was to uproot their entire sense of identity. I swallowed a lump in my throat. No wonder they looked so scared.

I stepped aside. "Come in," I said firmly. "And be welcome," I added in Old Slav.

Mittens wasn't a fan of his new roommates. I picked him up as he hissed at a pair of bearded domovois that poked at his dry food in curiosity before filling their flasks from his water bowl. Setting him on the counter, I scratched behind his ears.

"Be nice," I chided him. "They're our guests."

Looking at them all together, Zan's words sank in. Vyraj was in serious trouble. I drummed my fingers on the counter, and thought.

If this was just a fraction of the creatures fleeing their homes, how many were there? If even the domovois dared to abandon their nests, the other creatures must be truly desperate. The destruction in Vyraj was caused by instability in Nav. Zan wasn't sure, but I was. And if this Fern Flower was to blame, then the empty weirdness I'd felt in my pantheon made sense. How bad had it gotten in the days I've wasted arguing with Stonefield?

My fallen-in couch was now occupied by busy creatures that looked at the TV remote like it was a portal into another dimension. Looking self-important, Bava flicked on the screen, and the others cheered. Another kikimora was picking up my dirty socks from around the living room, looking as if she expected to get caught and scolded. Domovois are like brownies, they can't stand a mess. I snorted. They'd have their work cut out for them in my apartment.

I wasn't an axe-slinging warrior like Zan, but I had my talents. Finding things was one of them. And after Asmoday, the Spiral wasn't the only one after my talents.

I dug through my laundry until I found the card from last week. Between trekking through Underworlds and bickering with Stonefield, I had forgotten to file a complaint with the Legal team.

The three-headed dragon on the card was breathing fire into a kitschy inscription.

"Call me with a kiss."

Ridiculous. And what was more ridiculous was that I was going to do it.

Something was taken from the pantheon, and I require your assistance in finding it in the human realm.

Was he talking about the Fern Flower? If so, that was a whole sentence more informative than what Zan had told me, since he knew it hadn't been 'lost between the pantheons' but was somewhere in Yav. My secret admirer was willing to risk the Spiral's wrath—and do some morally gray shit—just to get my help. What else did he know?

Feeling like the cheesiest character in a fairytale retelling, I pressed my lips to the cool metal. The inscription flashed on and I could feel an inter-dimensional warp gather on the metal surface.

"This better work, you creep," I whispered. No way I was going to give him my address. Not that I would've minded seeing him zapped by my wards and immobile from the waist down. "Meet me at the Trinity Episcopal Cathedral, Reno, at ten a.m." Feeling foolish and desperate, I added, "Don't be late."

5

M Y GUN CARTRIDGES LOADED, I waited by the steps of the Cathedral. Like any good date, I was five minutes early and carried a knife in my boot. The blissfully fresh morning breeze carried over the Truckee River and cooled down my skin. I'd debated wearing a hoodie with my Docs, but decided that if I did that, Perun wouldn't have to gut me—I'd die of a heat stroke myself. Good thing there were camouflage spells, because no way I could hide my horns when I was this anxious. I've put plenty of monsters on their ass, but not knowing who this guy was put me at a serious disadvantage. Minutes ticked past ten a.m. and I began to doubt myself. What if I'd summoned him wrong? What if it took more than a few hours to get here from wherever he was?

The card in my pocket vibrated, and I pulled it out. Instead of "Call me with a kiss" another inscription flashed up at me.

It gave me an address.

I didn't have to walk very far. The smell of fried eggs filled my nose, and I was looking at the picturesque veranda of Smith and River, the local brunch joint. So, the girl-kidnapping creep had a penchant for fancy breakfast. Very interesting. I walked through the front door and was greeted by a pretty blond server who beamed at me from behind the checkout counter. A blast of air conditioner made me sigh with relief.

"Chrysoberyl Green?" she asked.

"Eh..." I wasn't sure how to take this newfound great treatment by the service staff. "Yes?"

"Right this way, please," she chirped. I followed her through the neatly lined side chairs and industrial decor toward the patio. Fresh air rolling from the Truckee River cooled my face. I surveyed the shaded tables that overlooked the sloshing waves and the romantic walkways. This felt more and more like a date. A very nice date. No wonder Jennie had walked right into his trap, silver pumps and all. Who was this guy?

We walked to the only occupied table on the veranda. Plates of appetizers and bottles of wine were arranged around the table. The man waiting for me glanced up at our approach and smiled.

His hair was a deep, glistening brown and curled around his ears and down the back of his neck. He wore a long caftan with golden stitching, and his shoulders were wide and his figure graceful. His black leather boots climbed up his muscular calves. He was gorgeous. As in the ridiculous, drop-dead kind of gorgeous that hit you in the gut. It did not impress me. If he was some incubus character, I had a gun-full of surprise for him. His deep green eyes lit as he took me in—tattered boots, tank top and all. He threw out his hand in a graceful gesture as if greeting an old friend and gave me a wide, delighted smile.

"Darling Chrysoberyl!" he announced, like he was an enthusiastic theater narrator announcing a new actor on stage. "Welcome!"

Old Slav accent tinged his every word, but it was so slight that I barely even noticed. I opened my mouth, but hesitated when I saw something unusual in his grinning face. It was his eyes—a green sheen zinged off his irises. I cocked my head and inspected him. To give Jennie some credit, he didn't look like a monster, but there was something, I don't know... lizardy about him. The way his body moved from one position to another—super fast. Rubies, emeralds, and golden coins lined the edges of his caftan and dotted his fingers. They would've looked ridiculous on any other man. I went still as I realized that the iron-shavings in my gun were entirely pointless. And so was every fire hydrant in this restaurant if he decided he wouldn't play nice.

He was a dragon.

The moment I realized it, he saw it in my eyes. His palms faced the air, and he shrugged, as if apologizing. There was only one zmei that lived in Nav and matched the description of a dandy playboy with a penchant for seducing beautiful women. What had Jennie called him? 'Gregory'? 'Gory' meant 'mountain' in Old Slav. I put two and two together.

"Zmei Gorynich," I whispered.

The beautiful man smiled. "Call me 'Grisha'."

"Why the theatrics?" I asked. "I'm sure, given your resources, you wouldn't have trouble finding my number."

He shook his head. "It was a regrettable necessity. Your father had forbidden the creatures of Nav to search for you. For the longest time, we didn't even know of your existence. Please," he gestured at the seat opposite him, "sit."

There was no point in playing coy. I'd come to him for information, and possibly, help. Feeling exposed, I sat in the comfy chair.

"Here you are," he said. "At last." His full lips pressed together in appreciation. "Just as I pictured you."

I realized he didn't magically sex Jennie up. He didn't have to. Charisma rolled off him like the beads of condensation on that expensive glass of wine in front of him. A three-headed dragon, he was infamous for starting various shit in Vyraj. Many ancient Slav warriors had tried to take him down for stealing a wife or a girlfriend. Some of the old tales and poems said they'd succeeded, and the others said he'd taken the women by force. Looking at him now, I decided that jealousy drove the pen of the poets. Gorynich—"Son of the Mountain"—just grew richer and more successful in turning ladies' heads. He was *old* old money. As far as ancient beings went, he was a skirt-chasing one-percenter.

A sigh over my head confirmed my theory as the server brought us a plate of crab cakes. She slid it over the table, making sure her cleavage was on full display while 'Grisha' eyed her appreciatively. Wow.

"Anything else I can get for you, Mr. Mountain?" she asked breathily.

"Thank you, darling," he purred. "That will be all."

Their exchange made me feel like I was interrupting something. I cleared my throat.

"Ah," he said, "forgive me. Anything else?" He gestured across the table that looked ready to break from the number of plates. "I wasn't sure what you liked."

I leaned back in my chair and put one of my scuffed Doc Martins on my knee. The dragon raised an eyebrow. Yes, much better.

"Thanks, I'm full," I said. Teeming with regret, the girl disappeared toward the restaurant. I tapped the table in front of me. "You wanted to find something in Yav," I said. "What is it?"

"Straight to business," he smiled. "How very American of you. It was something that was taken from my personal collection. Something that your father left in my possession while he rests." He took a sip of his wine.

I decided to not waste any more time.

"Is it the Fern Flower?" I asked.

His eyes widened as he choked on his wine. He swallowed with a shudder, and I suppressed a grin. I loved making arrogant ancients uncomfortable. Probably why I never got a promotion.

He tapped his chest and cleared his throat. "You're well informed."

I nodded, resigned. A part of me was relieved that I'd been right. The Fern Flower was the artifact that my "my secret admirer" had mentioned in his letter. The other part wasn't as relieved, knowing that the path to saving Zan's creatures—and my pantheon—would require me to go frolicking with this rich, pompous ass.

I narrowed my eyes. "You already know that it's in the human world," I said. "Why do you need me to find it?"

"You have a dragon inside you," he said. "Something that we have in common. From what I understand, your shifter form lends a special set of skills."

I nodded. "I can sense souls and herd them to their Underworlds." This wasn't anything he couldn't find out by asking around. "I just don't understand why you need my help in particular. Surely, you have access to all kinds of supernatural mercenaries and bounty hunters." The kind leading hellmutts, for example.

"What am I missing?"

His eyes darted to the restaurant staff who were whispering behind our line of sight.

"Don't worry," Grisha said. "They won't interfere. I've paid for the whole place until we're finished."

Of course he did. Cocking an eyebrow, I waited.

"The Fern Flower," Grisha's palms lifted in graceful supplication, "is a soul."

My eyebrows shot up my forehead. "What do you mean 'it's a soul'?"

"It's the soul of Nav," he said. "As living as the pulsing energy inside any human being. More alive, even. Without it, Nav is just—"

"A comatose body," I murmured. A surge of fear broke into goosebumps over my arms. Zan did not know how bad the situation really was.

Eyes going dark, he nodded. "Aptly put. To bring it back, a true child of Nav has re-infuse it with energy. And I don't know anyone who better fits this description than the daughter of its founding god."

I crossed my arms over my chest and leaned back in my chair. Grisha poured himself another glass and looked at me through the sunlit crimson liquid.

"In three days, the Flower will bloom on Ivana Kupala," at my confused look, he clarified, "the Summer Solstice. This is when the soul of Nav makes a connection to the rest of the pantheon. It has to be home when it does."

"And if it isn't?" I asked.

"The consequences will be... unpleasant."

Like the collapse of Nav and Vyraj with it?

I swallowed. "And you know where it is?"

"I do," he said.

"We have to report this to the Spiral, if we're so short on time," I said. "The sons of Perun are holding off the destruction. There are creatures fleeing Vyraj."

Grisha stiffened.

"We have to keep the inter-dimensional police out of this," his voice was strained. "They can't know where the Flower is."

My eyebrows shot up. "Why not?"

His face darkened, and his green eyes turned the color of poison. "Do you trust that everyone in your organization isn't so power-hungry they won't take a battery that strong for themselves?"

My mouth snapped closed at that. I tried to open it again and protest, but I couldn't. Grisha nodded.

"This is Nav business. With your help, we can get the Flower put back in time." He gave me an unreadable look. "If your father was awake, believe me, I wouldn't pull you into this business."

I crossed my arms over my chest. "Where is it, then?"

It was a while before he answered. "It's in your Yav city of Las Vegas," he said. "We have only one chance to take it. On the night that it blooms."

Vegas. That actually made sense. There were dragons there, lots of them. If someone had the balls to steal a treasure from Gorynich himself, they could do worse than locking it in the vault under the city.

"I doubt I can just find it," I said. "Even with my dragon's soul-searching GPS. How can you be so sure I could?"

"Because I know who took it," he said.

"Yeah?" I asked casually. "And who was that?"

"A beautiful woman," he answered. "Fiery and temperamental. Not unlike yourself." A smile touched his lips, and he took a drink of his wine. "Will you join me?" he said. "Just help me find it and bring it back. Then, you can go back to your life as a hero of the people, Veles' daughter."

I was tempted to tell this presumptuous ass to screw himself. Man, oh man was I tempted. Not only was he obviously not telling me something important, but pulling off something this big without informing the Spiral felt more dangerous than sticking your tongue into an electric socket. However, he was right. I couldn't exactly trust someone like Stonefield to help with this "little" problem without informing the other gods that my pantheon was unstable. Zan was holding down the fort, and this was my chance to help eliminate the damage. Another reason I couldn't refuse this guy was currently raiding my closet for cereal. Over fifty reasons, to be exact. What kind of a hero of the people would I be if I wasn't one for all the people?

"Okay," I said, finally. "I'll come with you to find the Flower."

"Wonderful!" He toasted me. "Our flight leaves in an hour."

Of course, he'd already booked the tickets. Like I said—a presumptuous, rich ass.

"Oh, no." A wicked smile stretched my lips. "If we're doing this, we're doing it my way."

6

The Crystallizer had been to literal Hell and back and came out looking like a million bucks. The purple paint job and the crystals and mushrooms looked like I had painted them yesterday. Parked in front of Grisha's fancy hotel, it looked like a graffiti on the side of a limousine. I grinned as I patted my darling beauty. Grisha looked exactly how I hoped he would—dumbfounded.

"I thought you wanted to get the lay of the land," I said innocently. "This road trip is going to make you feel like a real local."

Grisha eyed the van skeptically. Wearing a beige camp-collar shirt with golden dragons he'd paired with breezy linen pants, he looked like someone they'd try to rob at a local gas station. Although, I had to admit that his brown leather suitcase—that looked like something out of a period drama—gave me major luggage envy. My outfit was my favorite jeans, Docs, and a hoodie with the Buddha face. It made me look like his weed dealer.

"Does actually it drive?" he asked, incredulity in his voice. "Perhaps it saw its prime in the eighties?"

"Nineties," I corrected brightly. "This baby has seen some miles, and it will see many more. I jerked the door open and smiled at the fuzzy pink dice that dangled from the rear-view mirror. "Climb in."

He looked at me like I'd just suggested he kissed a frog on the off chance that it would turn into a princess. Man, I was loving this.

"It's not too late to fly first class, my darling," he gave me a pleading look. "What if your back aches after so many hours on the road?"

"It's only a few hours. Plus," I patted the wheel lovingly, "This little baby has a surprise under the hood."

It seemed to take a million years, but seeing my grin, Grisha realized he couldn't charm his way out of this one. Sorry I'm not Jennie, *darling*. Victorious, I swung the barn doors open, and he slid his suitcase between the green faux fur benches like he expected to never see it again.

"What is that smell?" he asked when we hit the road.

I breathed in the years of incense and weed.

"My childhood," I said with a grin.

I got us on the road and started driving north. The pleasure of listening to the ancient radio stutter over stations hummed through me. Since driving my ERS van was my primary method of transportation, I didn't get to drive the Crystallizer often. Speaking of ERS... I dialed Stonefield's number.

"Green," he said into the speaker. "I saw you take time off without consulting me."

"Director," I sang.

"Don't 'Director' me. How long are you going to be gone?"

"A few days, give or take." I shrugged. Or you know, forever, if Nav collapsed on top of me at a critical moment. What can I say, I'm an optimist.

"Where are you going, exactly?" he demanded. I could smell the smoke billowing off him from here.

"Just taking a road trip, Director, no real plan," I replied. "Going with a friend." Gorynich cocked an eyebrow at my friend-zoning him, so I added. "Not to worry, he's really low key."

"I don't care who you're with," my boss said. "Hrom tells me there's some worrying things happening in Vyraj. This isn't the time for you to go rogue."

"What do you mean?" I caught myself. "If you can elaborate, sir?"

"That information is above your pay grade," he ground out. "Return immediately, Green."

"I'm sorry, sir, you're cutting out," I ran my thumb over the speaker. "Losing signa—"

Satisfaction made me beam. I took the greatest pleasure of hanging up on him.

I glanced at Grisha, who had regained himself enough to recline in his seat like I was his personal chauffeur. Stonefield being cryptic and bossy wasn't new. The tinge of worry in his voice made me nervous. Normally, the djinn was pretty cavalier with my well-being.

"So, what's the plan?" I asked. "We're going to go find this woman and shake her down until the Fern Flower drops off?"

He shook his head. "There is an... event," he said. "We will attend it and find her there." Rolling down the window, he took a deep breath. "It's been a while since I've been to Yav. It's a lot drier than I remember."

That made curious. I didn't run into many supernaturals that didn't prefer Yav over their own pantheons. Mostly due to how easy it was to fool humans into being sustenance or playthings.

"You like it better than Nav?"

He shrugged. "Some years. However, Nav is home," he said. "I feel connected to it."

I thought of the hollow shadows under Zan's eyes. Some connection.

"I'm not a fan of other pantheons," I said.

He threw his arms over his head and slid his eyes over my profile. "Pity. It's not a bad thing to have more than one home."

"Is that what Yav is for you? A second home?"

"Of sorts," he said with a smirk. Even I had to admit that he had a sexy smirk. "My gold stretches much further here."

"I bet it does," I said dryly. What had I gotten myself into? I was taking the oldest party boy in existence to Las Vegas. This guy had more miles on him than the Crystallizer. "Who is this woman, then? Were you together?"

He pressed his thumb to his full lower lip, the gesture casually sexy. "She was my lover, yes." The touch of regret in his tone told me it had been serious. "I showed her everything, every bit of me, all my treasures. She betrayed me."

"What's her name?" I asked, not knowing what else to say.

"Delphyne," he said. "She is a dragoness."

Great, I thought, just what I needed. More dragons.

Three hours in, my bladder and the dipping gas level needle pulled me toward an exit. The helpful red sign proclaimed that there were 'GAS and SMOKES' in a small brown building that seemed to have grown out of the ground in the middle of nowhere. Bag of chips and Red Bull in both hands, I walked back to the car where Gory was pumping gas. Seeing how my checking account was in double digits, I wasn't too proud to let him pay for the fuel. We were in deep Nevada now. The blue strip of mountains lined the horizon and the exciting scenery of sage brush and wilted grass stretched down the never-ending asphalt roads. This late in the afternoon, the sun baked less like a forest fire and more like an oven. Small mercies.

We'd left late for a seven-hour road trip. Typically, I'd sleep in my van at a rest stop. Luckily, today I was spared the uncomfortable co-sleeping with the dragon. I smiled at the thought of what Uncle Ophis had installed under my old van's hood. I've been itching to press the "surge" button for miles. The jalapeño chips tasted extra good as I imagined how surprised Grisha would be at this fresh development in his travel plans. We'd get to Vegas in no time, easy-peasy.

Leaning on the van, Grisha entertained himself by making flames appear in his palm by snapping his fingers. Luckily, he was done pumping gas.

He smiled at my appearance. "Darling Chrys."

I opened my mouth to tell him to stop calling me "darling" when the afternoon sun dimmed over our heads.

My pulse leapt in animal panic. The dark swarmed around us with a beating of a thousand wings. Metal was sharp in my nostrils as a blackness fell around us. What the hell?

Chips dropping from my hand, I ran to the Crystallizer. I needed to get there before I lost sight of it. My Docs stomping down, I leapt over a parking separator. And promptly toppled to the ground.

To be fair—something had tripped me. Luckily, years of ERS training kept me from falling on my face. Rolling over my shoulder, I crouched with my gun whipped from its holster. Many somethings scattered out of the way with a flash of what looked like a carapace. The creatures were bugs the size of cats. Something no one has asked for, ever. This time, they weren't shy about slicing through my hoodie and the exposed skin on my wrists and cheeks. Shielding my face, I fired blindly into the swarm in front of me. The blackout hadn't been a coincidence. Somehow, the creatures had cast it for their ambush. I turned in a circle and fired iron shavings at every flash of a golden wing in the perimeter. Where the hell was the van?

Swearing, I searched for the souls in my vicinity. If Grisha was still by the van, maybe my dragon could find our way back to him. A chittering came from my right and I spun toward it. That's when tiny sharp teeth sank into my ankle. Luckily for my foot, my boots had protected it. I shot at the bug that had bitten me. Bullseye. With a metallic screech, it fell to the ground. Taking offense, its friends descended on me. My gun clicked in my hand, empty. They slashed and badgered me. I lost count of the cuts and bruises. There was a pull beneath my feet, as if the darkness wanted to swallow me down. I could no longer see my boots. Arms over my head, I sank to my knees.

Fire sizzled.

Grisha stepped out of the gloom like a human flame torch. Taking the opportunity, I fell to the ground and snatched my gun. His left arm extinguished, and he grabbed me across my torso. I could smell the burning fibers of my favorite hoodie. Damn it!

"Back to the van!" I yelled. "We need to get past them!"

Firing flames from his right hand like a human blow torch, Grisha dragged me backwards. I wasn't ashamed of the retreat. Something bug-like tearing into me in the dark through the sound of beating beetle-wings? No, thank you.

Grisha's back hit something, and we both came to a stop. With profound relief, I saw the purple paint of the Crystallizer's van doors and not the door to the gas station. Wait... the gas station!

"Stop the fire!" I yelled. "You'll blow up the whole thing! Go to the passenger side. I'll be fine!"

"Are you sure?" he asked. "My liege wouldn't be happy if I let his daughter be torn apart."

"I'll be happy if you end this trip without a body count," I said. "Go!"

Pushing out of his arms, I pushed toward the driver's seat. Damned buggies came at me with a vengeance. Grisha's fire had kept them at bay, but now they were back and more pissed than ever. What kind of bugs didn't die in a fire? Arms thrown over my face, I fumbled for the door. Bug bodies thudded against the window and the metal as I swung it open and slammed it behind me.

Swearing in Old Slav, Grisha jumped into the passenger seat. The beetles drummed against the metal and drowned out his words. The Crystallizer was as tough as an ERS van. I made a mental note to hug Uncle Ophis when I saw him. This wasn't the first his time his genius had saved my life. I pushed down the pedal and jerked the van forward. Not seeing the road wasn't good, but we needed to get out of the black cloud that made us blind. The bugs slammed into the window shield. Their carapaces left cracks in the glass. I prayed to all the gods we weren't about to run into a boulder.

Sun blinded me. The sudden visibility was disorienting. Flying past me, human drivers honked at the crazy lady barreling into the traffic in a purple van. I hit the brakes and spun the wheel to keep us out of an accident. Dust rising in the air, we screeched to a stop on the side of the road.

I shut off the engine and leaned on the wheel. My body buzzed with shallow wounds and I was afraid to look down to see how badly I was hurt. Death by a thousand cuts? That was a new one.

I dragged a sleeve across my face. "What were those things?"

"They came from Nav," Grisha said. "I've seen them inside the pantheon."

"What are they doing here?" I asked.

"Nav is coming apart," he said. His voice was heavy, and I glanced up at the dragon. His gold-threaded shirt was burned at the sleeves, but other than that, he looked like he'd just come back from a jog. Of course. "Without the Fern Flower, the entire place is out of sorts. Likely, they followed me here."

I gaped at him. "What would they want with you?"

He shrugged. "I don't know. My best guess is that they can sense the Fern Flower on me. They're seeking it out, same as us."

I looked down at myself. The Buddha face on my stomach gaped like he'd gotten a battle scar. I inspected the torn skin beneath. Half an inch more and I would be looking at a pile of guts on my lap. Hissing, I pulled my hoodie over my head. Cuts covered my forearms, growing less shallow where the cloth protected me.

"Thanks for your service, old friend," I said as I folded it on my lap.

Grisha eyed me appreciatively. What did I have to do to stop him from being a creep; literally die?

"You're welcome," he said. I fought hard not to roll my eyes. "Can we please call an airline now?" I couldn't help a smile at the pleading in his voice, not that I blamed him after that shit show. "I can chart us a private jet."

I shook my head. "Don't worry, next stop—Vegas." Ignoring the fact that I was smooshing my bloody chest in his face, I reached to the back seat. I pulled a clean black t-shirt out of my backpack. "No more delays."

"I—" he began.

"You're gonna have to trust me, or go search for the Fern Flower yourself," I said.

He pursed his lips, and I got the distinct impression that women rarely turned down his "generosity." Or argued with him. I was only too happy to help in his personal growth. Pulling the shirt over my head, I hovered my fingers over the surge button.

"Wait," I said. "I want to check something."

I drove the van back to the gas station. There, I searched the ground until I found what I was looking for.

"Gotcha," I said, satisfied. Grisha's fire couldn't take one down, but a round of iron shavings from a close range did the trick.

The bug was the size of my head and metallic, which explained the fire resistance. It had a small face with round eyes and its spindly legs splayed out over its belly.

The wings were razor-sharp. So were its pincers.

A large, clear gemstone was embedded in its belly. Marveling at the way it reflected rainbows from the sunlight, I ran my finger over its smoothness. Despite the metal, it looked totally organic, like the gold and silver fruit that grew on the trees in Nav. I didn't entirely buy the madness of the pantheon sending these things after us.

"What are you doing out here, you sharp little bastard?" I whispered. The bug didn't answer. Typical.

I shoved it into my backpack, and turned to Grisha. He looked at me expectantly, like he was already growing impatient with the lack of action. Oh, he was going to get some 'action' alright. Just not the type he'd hoped for. My lips stretching in a manic smile, I pushed the 'surge' button. Grisha's face turned green as the Crystallizer shot us through realities.

7

WE ARRIVED IN SIN City with the setting sun. Neon lights, lit up arches, and glowing signs filled our vision as we joined the never-ending traffic of the Strip. Giant billboards rolled over our heads. Show girls, liquor outlets, and comedians promising a "high-rollicking good time" competed for our attention. Rolling down the window, I let the delightful mixture of exhaust and cigarette smoke envelope us. Somewhere here, among the fool's gold, was the soul of my pantheon.

"Hey, mami!" Two guys in a rented convertible rolled up to us at the light. "You're looking fine! Wanna party or what?"

I gave them a wave, then flipped them a finger. Welcome to Vegas, baby.

Grisha tsked like a grandma. "Such disrespect! I'd never treat you this way."

"Yeah," I said dryly. "I know. You like to kidnap your dates first."

He looked outraged. "I only did it out of necessity!"

I gave a sidelong look. "Oh, yeah? You've never taken a woman from her home before? Or misled her into meeting you?"

He huffed. "Not without some serious green light from her end!"

I cocked an eyebrow. "What, like flashing an ankle?"

"I'll have you know—"

My phone chimed on the dashboard. Raising a finger to interrupt the dragon's chauvinistic Old-World outrage, I picked it up.

"Green," Rudy's voice came from the speaker. "Did you make it?"

"Yep!" I said brightly. "And in one piece! Well, almost."

I could practically hear him narrow his eyes. "What happened?"

Ignoring Grisha shaking his head in protest, I told him about the bugs. My partner humphed.

"Send me a picture," he said. "I'll take it to creatures' lab at the University and see if they can identify it."

It always weirded me out how the limbo realm of the Abrahamic world had an excellent university that reapers attended before working in Yav. I suppose with the amount of philosophers and geniuses that ended up there, it shouldn't be surprising.

"How's Purgatory?" I asked.

"Clean," Rudy said coldly. "I'm not used to it after hanging out in your apartment. I'm almost done with the unfortunate ass-kissing that every summit meeting is fraught with."

I grinned. Every once in a while, Rudy's language gave away his actual age—a number he'd never told me. From 'fraught,' I placed it somewhere around at least a hundred.

"I'll keep you posted," I promised before hanging up.

Grisha looked at me with mild disapproval. "Your partner certainly seems very curious about your whereabouts."

"Considering it's his part-time job to keep me alive," I said, "I imagine he's invested."

The dragon's watch flashed gold as he propped his chin on his fist. "A death deity invested in your well-being? You are fortunate." He pointed, imperious. "Pull in over here."

Two gilded towers rose on the other side of us against the setting sun and a winged golden lion over a flashing screen greeted us. The triangles of the romantic Gothic style studded delicate arches and bridges. My eyes went to the sign under the lion's paws. It read "The Venitian."

"You've got to be kidding me," I murmured.

Grisha gave me a wide a smile. "The Biggest hotel in America, my darling."

Despite the dragon's protests, I parked the Crystallizer myself. No way I was giving some twenty-year-old the keys to my precious. Not to mention that I didn't want him getting curious and pushing any buttons. A panicked valet suddenly ending up in California was not something I wanted to explain to Stonefield.

We stepped inside the glistening lobby and my eyes widened at the golden sphere positioned in the middle of the mosaic floor.

"Was this necessary?" I asked Grisha. "You're making us look like some high rollers on a grease fest. We're supposed to be keeping a low profile."

Grisha gave me a puzzled look, as if he couldn't imagine staying in Vegas any other way.

"This is the hotel I always stay in," he said.

"Yeah, this is how you get robbed of precious artifacts from your home pantheon," I pointed out.

He breathed in deep. "You smell that? Money and glamor."

I only smelled expensive cologne with the aftertaste of bleeding me dry of every dime, but to each their own. At least there was AC. The soles of my Docs had basically melted onto the sidewalk.

After the dragon flashed an impressive wad of cash, the hotel staff swarmed our luggage. An enthusiastic receptionist checked us in at the front desk. 'Mr. Mountain and his guest' were given the keys to the suite. Feeling like a smear of peanut butter on a velvet suit, I followed Grisha to the elevators. The bell boys had already disappeared with our stuff.

"They better not drop my bag," I mumbled, thinking of the muddy canvas that was holding on by a prayer. This whole thing was making me more and more uncomfortable.

Grisha placed his hands into his pockets, looking like a model of men's Country Club wear. "I don't know what you expected, darling," he said. "I'm not about to check my liege's daughter into a three-star hotel," he said that last bit with such derision that it was like I'd offered to sleep in a ditch.

"I was kind of thinking about a motel," I said honestly. The elevator doors opened, and we stepped into a hallway that was lit up like a runway. Or a path into an orgy club. "This feels like we'll have a target painted on our backs."

Grisha huffed.

"No one is going to let us attend the ball if we stay with the commoners," he said.

"Wait, what?" I gaped at him. "What ball?"

The bell boys greeted us with such enthusiasm that I nearly jumped out of my skin. They pushed open the door for us to step through, and my jaw dropped.

The suite dripped in gold, baroque tapestries, and polished oak furniture. Chandeliers hung over the dining room area and black table cloths were stitched with golden birds and flowers. The suite overwhelmed with opulence and luxury to such a degree that it seemed to fry my plebe brain all the way to my retinas.

"Holy shit."

Grisha extended his arm like a welcoming host at his private chateau.

"It's humble compared to my dwelling in Nav, but it serves the purpose when I come through this city."

I gave him a hard look. "Humble?"

He shrugged, unbothered. "The gold isn't real. I would never try to impress a woman like you with fake golden thread. Your rooms are this way."

"I have rooms?" I croaked.

I did indeed have rooms. Two, to be exact, and a walk-in closet that looked to be the size of my entire apartment. With a flourish and a grin, the dragon carried my scuffed duffle bag to the bedroom for me.

"There is a sauna if you'd like to rest," Grisha said. He blinked at the half-healed cuts on my cheeks. "You look… better."

I shrugged. "Demi blood." Reaching out my hand, I grabbed my duffle bag from his shoulder. "And I'm not going to the damned sauna. We have work to do."

"Of course!" he spread out his arms. "As you wish. I'll pour us champagne and we will plot. Please be at home here. Nothing is in excess for my liege's daughter." He gave me a curt bow. "I am but your vassal." He disappeared out of the door to give me privacy, or a moment to puke from excitement. I'm not sure what his usual experience with women was, but my money was on the latter.

"Some vassal you are," I murmured.

Gingerly, I sat on the edge of the bed and almost fell through. Damn if it wasn't the most comfortable bed I'd ever sat on. Lying back, I groaned. The overpriced mattress seemed to melt away all the aches I had from getting into a fight with the critters of Nav. A girl could get used to this. Wistfully, I wished my snooty ghost kitty was here. Mittens would love to have so much expensive upholstery to scratch. But then, I'd left him with my neighbor, Mrs. Lehmann. He was probably being spoiled rotten. I looked at the fancy baroque relief ceiling and wondered how deeply I was getting myself into trouble. Rolling to my side, I dialed Zan. The call dropped on the second ring, so he was probably still in Vyraj. I rubbed my face. I was afraid to imagine what was going on under the diamond sky of my home pantheon. How many more refugees had fled their homes? The son of Perun was one tough mofo, but his drawn face and hollow cheekbones told me stories I didn't want to hear. We weren't even together, and I felt like a military wife. With a groan, I made myself get out of bed. My aches and pains were back the second my feet touched the floor. I dragged my drowsy ass to the shower and made myself soak my wounds. Blood swirled in the drain. Slipping into a tie-dye shirt and a pair of black leggings, I went into the living room.

True to his word, Grisha had opened a bottle of champagne. The giant window that replaced the dining room wall showed the Strip. It stretched under us like a glittering centipede of lights. He wore a golden silk robe, his torso bare and his jeans were held up—precariously—by a belt with a giant golden buckle with the head of a dragon. He was lounging on the couch in a pose that gave Jeff Goldblum a run for his money. A glass of champagne fizzed in his dangling hand. I've never met Bacchus, but I was sure that the god of wine and revelry would die of jealousy.

"Chrys!" he said. The heat in his voice made me suspect it hadn't been his first glass. Or bottle, even. He poured golden liquid into a crystal flute. "Join me!"

"I'm good, thanks." Folding my feet under me, I sat on a couch in front of him. "How are we going to find your ex-girlfriend?"

He cocked an eyebrow. "Wherever do you find a beautiful, rich woman? A dance, of course! We will attend the annual Conflagration Ball. Delphyne is sure to be there."

I regarded him. "Sorry, I left my glass slippers at home."

Sweeping back the curling hair off his forehead, he gave me a wink.

"That won't be an issue, I assure you." He set down his glass, sobering. "We have other concerns in this matter."

And there it was, the other shoe dropping. "What concerns?"

Letting out a long sigh, he draped both arms over the back of the couch. A weaker woman would be tempted to stare at his sculpted bare chest. Not me, of course.

"This is a dragon ball that happens in Las Vegas every summer," he said. "In the past, I made every one, when this city wasn't shy about being run by your human mafia." At my questioning expression, he clarified. "Vegas' first dragons, of course. Since then, certain actions—misunderstandings—led me to become a kind of persona non grata."

I snorted. "Slept with the wrong wife?"

He grimaced. "Crassness doesn't compliment your stunning face."

"Good to know," I said. "So now what? How do we get in?"

"I plan to negotiate my way in," he said. "The gatekeepers at the ball will not withstand the power of my dragon form." He said it with a casual cockiness that told me he really wanted me to believe that it was true.

I narrowed my eyes. "You're planning to break and enter a ball full of dragons?" I asked. He shrugged and poured himself another glass. I wondered if the dragon flames inside his body would finally catch on the booze and set the couch on fire. "Call me old-fashioned, but I don't think that storming the castle with only two soldiers is good for our health."

"Your father entrusted the Fern Flower to me," he said. "Delphyne should've known better than to steal it."

"Right." His entire plan wasn't so much a plan as a recipe for disaster. "Can we just steal the tickets?"

He gaped at me, then let out a throaty laugh. "Steal from the dragons. Are you mad, woman? Even if we did, they personalize each invitation to the invitee's spiritual signature. Trying to use them at the door to the Ball is suicidal."

I tapped my foot on the floor. "But it could be done? The stealing?"

He shrugged. "I have three heads, and I'm not crazy enough to try."

Grinning widely, I leaned back in the couch. "I think I might know someone who is."

8

The Venitian's early morning crowd was made up of families and disgruntled drunks being dragged along by their excited wives to the glitzy shops of the giant hotel. I couldn't help but gawk—the damn hotel was literately a small city. The ceiling, painted like the sky that stretched over the 'streets' of quaint Italian homes, gave a strange illusion of being outdoors. Every once in a while, I'd forget that we were actually inside. We grabbed breakfast crepes at one of the dozens of picturesque shops and I felt my spirits lifting. I suspected the dragon took me down a scenic route, since there was no way the hotel took so long to walk. Did it? Last time I was in Vegas, my mom and I stayed at a friend's ranch just outside the city. We went to the Strip just for a buffet that overwhelmed me with tourists and middle-aged men that stared at my teenage curves a little too long. This was like walking inside of a toy box.

Grisha read my expression correctly. "Impressive, isn't it?" He was wearing a red button-up shirt that accentuated his toned body instead of hiding it. I tried not to roll my eyes as women—and men—stared. Although a grandma who gave me a thumbs up behind the dragon's back made me grin. "I love coming out to play in Yav. And the humans! What a delightful bunch they are."

"We are," I murmured.

He cocked an eyebrow. "Do you not count yourself among the gods?" he asked. "It would be the more flattering way to go. It definitely has more perks."

I tucked a strand of hair behind my ear. "Human fits me better," I said. "I'm only in my twenties. Eternal beings..." I shivered, trying to forget what I'd experienced with Clementia. "They don't care. Life doesn't mean much to them."

Grisha gave me a contemplative look. "It is hard to value something you see come and go so much. If you become too attached to something as fleeting as human life, you will find your heart broken again and again."

I blinked at the profound statement. "Have you lost a lot of loved ones?"

"Too many to count," he said. "But it doesn't mean I don't value life. Every one of them was precious to me. Love is something you find and lose, again and again."

I bit my lip. Suddenly, the dragon didn't seem like a shallow representation of everything wrong with the eternal pantheons.

"I'm sorry," I said.

He shrugged and gave me a panty-dropping smile. "That's why I'm always searching for a wife I will not outlive."

Narrowing my eyes, I gave him a hard look. "You don't seem to have trouble finding mortal girlfriends while you search."

He laughed. "I've lived a long time, darling. Do mortals not have hobbies?"

"Breaking hearts is not a hobby," I said. "It's a bad habit."

"They will remember me well," he said. "I've always left them... satisfied." The look that he gave me made color rise to my cheeks. It had been entirely too long since I'd had anyone in my bed. Naughty dreams about Zan notwithstanding. "Isn't that what matters?"

I couldn't help but laugh. "You're shameless."

"I am what I am." His voice was light. "And you are a goddess. Perhaps you don't feel it yet, but Nav belongs to you. Along with my devotion."

Now, he was laying it on thick.

"I grew up in a van," I said. "Nav doesn't belong to me." I eyed his tall, masculine figure. "And you're definitely barking up the wrong tree."

He grinned. "If you say so."

We walked past the canals dotted with gondolas. The pools stretched between the overpriced shops that sold fancy chocolate, gelato, and, for whatever reason—oxygen. The azure waves under the blue, cloudy 'sky' were dotted with gondolas manned by singing gondoliers wearing blue-striped shirts. I was losing track of all the shops as they rolled by us. As we walked away from the Venetian portion of the hotel, and into the Palazzo, the walkway took us to escalators that connected the two portions of the giant structure. Here, a small oasis of green plants and flowers circled a shimmering pool. A waterfall fell between the two escalators, and in front of it stood a red sculpture. It was four letters that rose twenty feet tall.

LOVE.

I grinned widely. This was a famous sculpture that had appeared at Burning Man. My mother had taken many photos in front of it, and I had one framed in my apartment. It was like a wave from a friend in the sea of attention-draining luxury. Suddenly, I felt steadier on my own two feet.

In the mouth of the 'O' a familiar figure rested their back on one side and their feet on the other. They were wearing brown check pants and a white tank top that showed off their toned, androgynous body. Orange hair was pulled back into a short ponytail, and I saw a glimmer in the air. Handy, the shimmering mage hand, was just camouflaged enough to not draw the attention of the human passersby. Its master turned their head toward me and gave me a wide grin.

"Doll Face," Tick said. "I thought you'd never call."

"You're trying to break into the Conflagration Ball?" The trickster barked a laugh. "With this fop?" They gestured a gelato spoon in Grisha's direction. "You'll never make it through the door."

"And who are you, to call a judgment as outrageous as this?" He looked at me. "Are you sure that this *half* demon can help, darling?"

I suppressed a sigh as Tick's face turned predatory. "Yeah, *darling*," Tick drawled. "Who am I to help this tourist that couldn't tell a hustle from stuffing twenties into a bra? I am so out of my depth."

The dragon narrowed his eyes at Tick. He was lounging in a chair in front of the ice cream shop where Tick had insisted they needed some sugar to help them "think better." Last night when I'd called them, they were overjoyed at my appearance on their home turf, and eager to help. Or, I suspected, to show off their skills in familiar territory. Now, I wondered if I had underestimated the force of Tick's and Grisha's collective egos. The dragon propped up his elbow and rolled his shoulders. Big, intimidating male. Yeah, like that was going to work.

I raised my hands. "Everyone, behave!" I turned to Tick. "Look, Vegas is your territory. That's why I called. You know it better than anyone."

They took another bite out of their cotton candy-flavored gelato. "You better believe it."

"Grisha..." I gestured toward the dragon. "Needs to find someone inside. I need to follow them to see what they're hiding. This is about Nav and the instability the missing Fern Flower is causing. If I can sense it, I can find it and bring it back." I dropped my eyes to the table.

"Zan is in trouble, and there are so many creatures fleeing."

Tick groaned. "You're still carrying a torch for that jock?"

Grisha gave me a sharp look. "What jock?"

I waved my hand. "Zan and his brothers are holding down the fort in Vyraj. They're on the upper levels fending off the unstable elements that are tearing the pantheon from beneath." Tapping my finger on the table, I gave Tick a hard look. "If I don't return the flower by the Summer Solstice, it won't matter how strong they are. Nav will collapse, and those that survive will be homeless. My father... I'm not sure he'd been able to make it out of the roots."

They sobered. "That's quite the time crunch."

I held their eyes. "And the ball is tomorrow night," I said. "Can you sneak us in?"

There was a beat where I wasn't sure that the trickster wouldn't simply disappear and take their ice cream with them. Finally, they scratched their head.

"Damn it, Chrys," Tick said. "Why you gotta be so suicidal all the time? Your friends need a break every once in a while, you know."

I smiled. "That's rich coming from you. Have you paid off that debt yet?"

They grimaced. "Not exactly. Which is why I can't be seen anywhere near the Ball. I love you, Doll, but I'm not getting fried alive."

Grisha snorted. "How convenient. Just tell us the truth that you can't find the tickets, demon spawn."

The look that Tick gave him was so full of venom, I was surprised the humans walking past didn't drop dead.

"That's not what I said." They dragged their eyes from the dragon. "I can get you tickets, but it won't do you much good."

"Why not?" I asked.

"The Conflagration Ball is by invitation only, and your boy here isn't invited," they said in a mocking tone. "Gee, I wonder why."

"Tick," I warned.

The trickster shrugged. "If you're not the intended guest, they're spelled to kill anyone who tries to step through the gate." They ran their finger over their throat. "By blowing their heads off."

Grisha grunted, agreeing with them for once.

I swallowed. "Is there a way to break the spell?"

Tick shook their head. "They have some seriously powerful witches casting spells in this city. Lots of protection juju, as you can imagine."

I chewed on my lip. "But you can get them, the tickets?"

Tick shrugged, and Handy wiggled its shimmering fingers from their shoulder. "With a bit of skill and camouflage magic. I know a couple of high-rollers who were invited. They wouldn't be hard to lift." They gave Grisha a wide grin. "For me."

"So," I said. "You'll do it?"

"Are you going to break in with the Crystallizer otherwise?" they asked. They knew too well from our spring road trip what the van was capable of. They sighed at my "innocent" expression. "Fine. For you, I'll do it for free," they said. Their head cocked as they regarded Grisha. Over their shoulder, Handy rubbed its thumb and forefinger together. "But it will cost the insufferable lover boy some hot cabbage."

Before I could open my mouth, Grisha shrugged and reached inside his shirt. He pulled out a wad of cash and tapped it in front of the trickster.

"Will a thousand American dollars suffice?" he asked.

"You know what?" They gave me an approving nod and snatched the cash. "He's actually growing on me."

To kill time, Grisha and I wandered the shops in search of a dress for me. I became convinced that the dragon had some sort of charisma magic on his side. As soon as we walked through the door, the stony stares of the cashiers turned into an eagerness. It's like they could smell the money on him. Maybe I should get rich, I thought as I watched the girl at Louis Vuitton fawn over the handsome man. It seemed to open a lot of doors. And it wasn't like I wasn't already pissing off pantheons full of monsters. We went from store to store and every time I shrugged into a glittery, strippery abomination that rode up my butt and gave my non-existent bosom a facelift, I grew more impatient.

"I'll just wear a button up," I said. "What's the harm?"

Grisha actually paled. "Absolutely not! I will not have my reputation lose its shine over a badly dressed date."

"I thought your reputation couldn't get any worse," I needled. "For your general sluttiness and all."

He ignored me as he pulled me along into a yet another shop full of shimmering gowns.

"They really look all the same to me, Grisha," I complained. "I'll just wear an illusion or something—"

A pair of sandals drew my attention. They were silver heels that were studded with blue gems, up and down the delicate straps that looked meant to be wound up all the way to the knees. The heels were carved into a shape of twigs, and gods were they gorgeous. I couldn't tear my eyes away and that's how Grisha found me—staring.

"They are beautiful," he said. "I think I understand where your mind is with this."

He snapped his fingers and the store clerk actually ran over instead of slapping him.

"Find her size, please," he said to the flustered girl who looked ready to pass out.

The price tag slipped from under the sole and my eyes widened.

"No way—"

Grisha gripped my shoulder. "I know the perfect dress," he breathed into my ear. "Wait here."

I waited while the girl fell over herself, getting the fit of the shoe just right. When she handed me the gorgeous bow-decked gift bag, Grisha was back. He carried a box under his arm.

"I think we're ready," he said. He looked very pleased with himself.

"What did you get?" I tried to gather the brand from the box.

"It's a surprise," he said.

I crossed my arms over my chest. "I don't like surprises."

"I'll tell you." He beckoned me forward until I leaned in. "You'll look like a goddess," he whispered. "But that's hardly a surprise."

Back in our suite, we unloaded our purchases, and I tried my best not to feel too anxious while I waited for news from Tick. Not that I doubted the Trickster—they were a clever and skilled thief—but I wasn't sure what was going to come next. Cleansing spells weren't something I was good at. Or any spells at all.

After a restless nap in my ridiculously posh bed, I woke up with Grisha pacing in the suite dining room. The hotel staff had laid a gorgeous dinner out for us—ribeye steak, salmon fillets on a bed of vegetables, and slices of chocolate cakes. It made my mouth water. The dragon hadn't even bothered with a flamboyant change of clothes and still wore his red shirt. That told me he'd paced all the way through while I'd napped. Grabbing a bottle from the table, he poured himself a glass of wine. I passed on the alcohol, but took my time enjoying the dinner the best I could. My rattled nerves didn't make it easy.

By sundown, the tables had been cleared along with Grisha's patience.

"This demon spawn of yours hasn't shown," Grisha's voice was tight. "I imagine they've spent the day gambling with my money."

I shrugged. "If they did, they've tripled it. Push comes to shove, we'll use the van." Regarding him, I tried to read his expression. "And really, I trust them more than I trust you."

He drank his wine, eyes sparkling green in the candelabra light. All of a sudden, I knew gutturally that he could fry me on the spot. "I am a man, and you are a woman. That is probably wise."

I cleared my throat, not liking the "man—hunter, woman—prey" implication in his tone. "I can take care of myself."

He smiled in a way that made me warm all over. "Undoubtedly. Who is this Zan that Tick referred to? A boyfriend?"

"None of your business," I said lightly. "As long as we're waiting for Tick, I need to make a call. There has to be a way to break the curse on the invitations."

In my room, I dialed a number I knew by heart. My mom answered from the first ring.

"Nathair Bhig," she said, using my nickname. 'Little snake'. "How are you? Is everything okay?"

Her concern warmed me like a hug. I gave her a brief rundown of the situation—taking out the life-threatening parts, of course.

Since Sarah May Green was many things but not a fool, she got straight to the point.

"If there's a curse on your friend's item, then they need to perform a purification ritual. You could do it with a rune, of course, but—"

"I'm not as good as you," I said to her. "And my friend doesn't have that kind of time."

There was a long silence on the other end, punctuated by my mom's wife, Shelly, asking her where she'd put the "good stuff," whatever that meant.

"Do you remember the shrine between Flamingo and Caesar's Palace?" I grunted affirmation, and she went on. "There is more than one reason we stopped by there every time we passed through. There are few places in Vegas to cleanse your aura, and the spirit inside will consume the extra energy."

"That's it?" I asked. "Come and pray at the shrine?"

I could almost hear her smile. "Is anything free, honey? Tell them to bring silver. For a small curse a coin would do, as a payment for clarity."

And for a death curse? I wanted to ask, but didn't. Instead, I thanked her and hung up. Something told me that a coin wouldn't do for a curse that wanted off with my head.

9

"It took a bit of hustle," Tick said, voice haughty. "But we pulled it off. Took these off some bougie start-ups from New York. Dude had to take a piss in MGM Grand between slamming whiskey sours and Handy waited in the toilet bowl." The mage hand high-fived them. "Amateurs."

"Gross." I took the black envelope with a lot more hesitation than when I thought it was *just* going to blow our heads off. "No wonder the CIA is after you."

The trickster grinned. "Actually, the CIA isn't. But basically everyone else is."

I shook my head. If the Spiral ever got their hands on them, it would mean some serious dungeon time. Or one hell of an employment opportunity.

Grisha inspected the envelope so thoroughly, I thought he was going to give it a sniff.

"These are... legitimate," he said unhappily. "I'm impressed, demon."

Tick grinned. "I'm not just a pretty face."

"I'm going to the shrine today," I said to them. "Once they're cleansed, we can find Delphyne and track her down."

"Are you sure?" Grisha said. "This will be dangerous."

"I'm a big girl," I told him. "Can tie my own Docs and everything." I took the envelope back from him. Inside, even I could sense the slithering pulse of something wrong. The paper was saturated with something menacing that wanted to be released. I felt an itch at the top of my head and agreed with my dragon—the spell wanted us to steal the invites. It wanted to kill us. My mom was right, as always. Suddenly, I felt like I had no business tangling with something so evil. I was out of my depth, but my companions didn't need to know that. Flashing Grisha a confident smile, I said, "I'm my father's daughter, am I not?"

A green shimmer ran over his pupils. "Yes, you are," he said simply.

Hell has nothing on Vegas in July. In the egg-frying heat of the afternoon, I began walking to Caesar's Palace. My mind was as clear as it was going to be after I did my best to perform a warrior's cleanse in the suite's sauna. My gun was at my hip. The entity I was about to go see didn't play games when it came to testing metal. I'd left my jacket in my room, taking my backpack instead. A long, silver dagger that Rudy had gifted me months ago went on top of a sweatshirt that covered the weird bug from Nav. A steampunk beetle wasn't something I wanted hotel's housekeeping to discover.

My phone buzzed in my pocket and I looked down to see Stonefield's profile picture. I pressed "ignore." Whatever my "smoking hot" boss wanted, it could definitely wait.

The heat kept people clustered at the entryways of the casinos with iced margaritas in their hands. Only the guys shoving escort cards at tourists and the leggy women dressed like show girls were out and about, but they were a stronger breed than me. I was starting to think I was going to evaporate out of my skin and dissolve into the universe on my short walk past the pink lily of the Flamingo hotel. I gave a guy playing guitar under a sun umbrella five bucks for the honesty of his sign that read "I want beer." Anyone who learned to play an instrument just to support their bad habit was alright in my book.

Up the escalators and down the bridge brought me to where I needed to be—the Brahma Shine. I downed a now-warm Red Bull I'd brought from the hotel. My boots stomped down the sweltering stairs and toward the smell of incense.

Despite my mother's best efforts, I'm not the meditating type. I think my heart just beats too quickly from the caffeine. But as soon as I stepped into the area of the shrine, all the noise of the city receded. The shrine itself had been in Las Vegas since the eighties, and its aura seemed to repel the smoke-saturated, copper-and-olive smell of the city. I took the dagger from the backpack and slid it into the holster at my hip. The incense smoke permeated the air and immediately calmed my spirits. Like all places of heavy worship, the energy of human thought and prayer reached the land around it and deep into the ground. I can't see in the magical spectrum, but I imagined the shrine glowed. I knelt on one bench and lit my incense stick. Looking up at the face of Brahma that was framed with yellow flowers, I focused my intent on seeing past the golden features of the faraway god. My dragon inside me was quiet. This was not the place for the dead, but a place for living energy. The silver dagger at my hip poked into my thigh and I shifted, uncomfortable. When I looked back up, I was no longer in front of the shrine.

Grey smoke filled my vision and made my eyes water. "Hello?" I called.

I was hotter than ever, and I swear I could feel flames touch the edge of my boots. Then, I felt something else. A cool blade at my throat.

"Who are you to enter my In-Between?" A melodic voice asked in my ear.

I swallowed. I had expected this, of course. But the smoke and the dizziness and disorientation had taken me by surprise. It's dangerous to meddle with elementals, and this one had been feeding on the greed and the incense for years. Fire elementals take wrath and frustration and all the negative energy into themselves. People walking away from the shrine feel purged for a reason. It's a magic as old as worship places go.

"I've come seeking purity," I said. "A spell purged from an item."

"Hmmm." The elemental's hot breath scorched my ear. "Are you worthy of purification?"

I made myself stop reaching for the dagger at my hip. "I am," I said.

There was a rustling of smooth silk robes and a sudden absence around me.

"We shall see," the voice rustled. A stone altar appeared in front of me. "Place the item you want to cleanse there."

Stepping toward the pedestal, I placed the black envelope down. Red seeped off the edges like the invites dripped poison. I grimaced at the disgust that clenched my stomach. Death magic was scary. And when a spell was placed by a heavy weight—like the freelance witches of Las Vegas—the result was downright nasty. My mouth tasted bitter.

The delicate shadow let out a melodic sigh.

"Ah. And do you know the price for this cleanse?" she asked.

I nodded. "I do."

Her lips—I was now sure it was a woman—were suddenly close to my ear. "So be it."

In an instant, she and the altar were gone. Smoke crawling on the ground rose, darkened, and separated. Humanoid shapes that hulked over me like men over six feet tall. They took a wide, hostile stance. I dropped my backpack to the ground and my hand whipped out my dagger. In such close quarters, using my gun seemed entirely pointless. The dagger did, too, but the cool of silver encouraged me. It had been a while since I'd trained with Rudy, but I felt my stance widening with remembered surety. Zan and the domovois weren't even the worst of it. Countless creatures would die and lose their homes if I didn't get into that ball. Palm sweaty around the hilt, I waited until the first one attacked. Ducking under his reach, I stabbed the figure in the ribs, under his armpit. There was a hiss that sounded like something between a cat and a sizzling pan, and the figure fell to the side. I rolled out of the way of an oncoming swing from another smoky assailant and slashed through its arm. I don't know what I expected—some sort of resistance, maybe? Instead, my dagger sliced through the smoke. My momentum carried me forward, and I barely caught myself. A roll that was trained into me spared me the cold floor and a broken nose. When I came up for air, I saw that I'd hardly made a dent. In fact, I hadn't made a dent. The smoky shadows crowded my vision, and I saw cold steel and glowing embers for eyes. At that moment, I recognized what they were.

"Ohhh, shit," I breathed.

Smoke golems. Years ago, I'd run into them in Lilith's realm. Run was the key word there. My partner at the time—a pasty-faced young necromancer—didn't know the barrel of the gun from the grip. It became very clear to me that even my scrappiness wasn't enough to break through a force that was literally invincible. We made it out on foot and summoned the van that got us out of the realm in the nick of time. I didn't have my van here. The only thing I had was a silver dagger and the now useless ability to see and manipulate souls. Just to be certain, I felt around the room in search of anything I could attack with my dragon. As predicted, the only thing waiting for me was emptiness. The golems had no souls. No physical bodies, either. The smoke fairy's words came back to me, sounding that much more ominous.

"Do you know the price for this cleanse?" Oh, I think I got it now.

The golems seemed to delight at my sudden realization. Breaking format, they flanked me. Their eyes burned inside the blobs that served as their heads, and the swords in their hands were entirely real. Steel sang over my head, and slashed at my sides. I parried where I could, but mostly, I tried to not get hit. There were too many of them. Sweat rolled into my eyes as the heat rose in the room, as if someone had opened a door to the merciless heat of Vegas. The smoke made my eyes water. With lessened visibility, I lost footing. There wasn't much I could do but to try to survive. Maybe the fairy put a time clock on how long I could last? She didn't actually expect me to kill them, right?

A sword slashed me across my ribs, and I howled in pain. I clutched the dagger in my hand and fell to the ground. Here, the air was cooler and cleaner. My teeth clenching over pain, I rolled out of the way of swords that came down towards me. The pain cleared something in my head. I pulled up my feet as I took a chance at an opening and broke out of the throng of smoking shadows.

The golem's limbs might've not been corporeal, but there was something that held the monsters together. Elementals needed a spark of life. And whenever there was a spark, there was a way to put it out. I whirled around on the approaching shadows. They didn't seem in a hurry. That made sense, since they fully expected to kill me. I wiped sweat and blood off my forehead and made myself think.

Their eyes glowed, and the thickness over their torsos suggested something like a core. Maybe my mistake had been to go for their heart. It would make sense if their heart wasn't where the human one would be. My eyes flicked to the middle of the closest smoke golems. I watched the smoke move over its form until something caught my attention. There, deep within its stomach, was a flicker of an ember. I didn't wait. I didn't think. With a guttural scream, I pounced on the monster.

I'm not sure if it was my boldness that caught him off-guard or my stupidity, but the golem froze for just a moment too long. My dagger bore into its stomach. The blade dove in without resistance, and for a moment, my heart sank. Then it hit something solid. I closed my eyes and twisted. The already familiar hissing came from the creature. I plunged deeper into the solid matter. It was smaller than the size of my fist. With a sickening crunch, it split in half. The smoke that comprised the creature cleared and something clanked on the floor. I blinked at the round lump of coal. It was black and orange, with a dying flame. Triumph jolted through me.

I'd killed a smoke golem! Take that, Stonefield.

The other creatures hissed among themselves. I could feel the tension rise with the heat that pressed against my skin. Please, let them think I wasn't worth the risk. Of course, they did the opposite. Swords flashed and my vision blurred.

I parried and ducked. Falling back, I let another sword glide off the hilt of my silver dagger. The creature fell over me and re-formed behind my back. I spun and let instinct take me to its core. This time, I didn't hesitate when I hit something solid. My dagger halved the coal that kept it alive. I panted, a grin wide on my face. I could do this—I could get the invitations cleansed without paying the price that demanded.

My foot kicked one half of the coal. It was all that was left of the golem I'd killed first. Smoking, it skittered across the stone floor. A shape thickened over it and my heart sank. Something was wrong. Very wrong. Whooshing from behind me, a sword sung toward my shoulder. Instinct made me fall to the side. It was the only thing that saved me from a severed arm. Sharp pain blazed across my bicep. Spinning around, I looked into the eyes of the thing that I already expected to see—the golem reborn from the shard of his life coal. I didn't need to turn around to know that the thickening at the edge of my vision was another piece of coal turning one monster into two. Smoky saliva was thick on my tongue. I was so *so* screwed.

There were simply too many of them as they bore me to the ground. I felt steel pierce my ribs and my thighs. I smelled blood. My blood. I was going to die here, I realized. Stabbed to death by some incorporeal bastards who didn't even have the decency to perish when I killed them. I called to my dragon and she uncoiled uselessly in my chest. Even if I turned into my toothy counterpart, I couldn't kill literal fucking smoke. Fern Flower would be lost and thousands of innocent Nav creatures would die. And Zan— Zan.

"No," I gasped. "Nav, please—"

Something warm filled my limbs, and I wondered if that's what death felt like. My tongue was thick as I saw a sword rise over my head. I had never felt much toward my home pantheon. Unlike Zan, I didn't grow up there. But now I felt its magic stir within me. In my mind's eyes, I saw golden apples swinging in the breeze, smelled the green grass and the saw the speckled black sky that wasn't really a sky. Something thudded inside me. The golems' eyes flared and the fist sword fell down. My eyes flew shut.

With a sound like a clattering bell, something ricocheted off the steel. I opened my eyes to see the golem's sword skittering across the floor. The smoky monster looked as confused as I did. A buzzing of metallic wings was its only warning. With a flash of gold, the bug I'd brought with me bore into its center. Unlike my dagger, it didn't split the coal that was its life. It pulverized it.

If the golems had mouths, their jaws would have hit the floor. Swords lifted off my body. The steampunk beetle made its rounds through the monsters. It didn't even look like it bothered to evade the weapons. Hitting their cores, he reduced each one to a pile of dust with a fancy blade on top. I scampered up to a crouch and clutched my palm around the hilt of my silver dagger. What the hell was going on?

When there was nothing in the room except was a handful of coal dust, the bug darted toward me. I shielded my face, but it simply paused mid-air. Up close, I could see the shredded carapace where my gun had grazed it. Apparently, it wasn't enough to kill it.

Lucky for me.

Its beady eyes turned in its sockets expectantly.

"Ah," I mumbled. "Thanks?"

With a deafening buzz, it was gone. I blinked at the space it used to be. What just happened?

A stone pedestal rose in the middle of the room. The invitations were still lying there.

"You've passed," the voice that came from everywhere sounded irritated. Out of the corner of my eye, I saw a sliver of a beautiful pale face and a swish of a crimson robe. It was gone when I turned to look at it. "Take your prize."

Flames consumed the invites, and I gasped. Then, the fire was gone as instantly as it appeared. When I picked up the black envelope, the paper was just that—paper. No sense of foreboding dripped from its pages.

The bug had torn through the side of my backpack. I slid the invites and the silver dagger into its depth and clutched it to my chest. When I looked up, the Vegas sun blinded me once again. I stood outside the shrine, covered in blood and reeking of smoke.

10

"**W**HY ARE YOU ALWAYS covered in blood?" Tick asked. They turned to Grisha who was already dressed to the nines in a silver suit that complimented his tan and green eyes. Standing against the panoramic view of the sun gilding the sky scrapers, he looked exactly like what he was—a drop-dead gorgeous billionaire. "You'll have to sponsor a whole new wardrobe for this psycho."

I put the invites on the table in front of them. Only then, I allowed myself to sink into the couch, blood and all. Expensive upholstery be damned. After what I'd just been through, Grisha could shell out for cleaning. My bicep had got the worst of it and I leaned away from the arm rest to make sure I wasn't going to get glued to the fancy fabric. In the perfumed air of the suite, I could smell the reek of smoke on my clothes and skin. It was a Vegas miracle that no cop had apprehended me as I'd stumbled back to the Venitian.

"It's done," I said.

Grisha paced past me and picked up the envelope. His eyes widened.

"You are incredible!" He grabbed my knuckles and kissed them. "My trust was not misplaced!" His eyes scanned me from my coal dust-covered Docs to another ruined shirt. He grimaced. Rolling their eyes, Tick disappeared in the direction of the bathroom and appeared minutes later with a first aid kit.

Their impish face pinched with concern as they slid onto the couch next to me.

"Don't worry," I said. "A quick shower and I'll be ready to party."

"Shut up," the trickster said.

Handy was already opening the latches on the plastic box. Its nimble fingers pulled out gauze and bandages and placed them in Tick's waiting hand. As they rolled up my sleeve, I watched Grisha out of the corner of my eye. At first, I'd wanted to tell him about the bug. He knew more than I did about Vyraj, after all. Maybe he knew why the creature had turned from an attacker to a defender. But something about the shrine had cleared my senses enough to understand this: my gracious Vegas host was definitely hiding something.

"So," I winced as the trickster dabbed my wound. "Have you tried contacting Delphyne?"

He pursed his lips. An emotion like regret flashed across his face. It didn't look right on his arrogant features.

"Yes," he said. "She will not pick up my calls."

"What happened between the two of you, anyway?" I asked.

He spread out his hands. "Delphyne is a mercurial creature. She lived with me in Nav, and we had—" A lusty smile stretched his mouth. "A beautiful time. And then one day, she changed her mind. A womanly madness came across her."

"Oh," I said innocently. "Did she go *crazy* on you?" Tick and I exchanged a meaningful look.

He looked back at me, oblivious to my sarcasm. "Yes, indeed. To this day, I don't know what prompted her to betray me."

"Aha." I rolled my now bandaged shoulder. Next, he was going to tell me that women "were a mystery."

"Have you tried, I dunno, actually listening to her?"

"Of course!" he looked aghast. "Every word that dropped from that beautiful mouth. She left me for no reason I could possibly perceive."

I rubbed the bridge of my nose. Was there a couples' therapy in Nav? Maybe Grisha could go into a single session for a little while. A hundred years or so would do.

"Are you telling me that our pantheon is falling apart because of 'no reason'?" I pressed.

He shrugged. "Women are a mystery," he said magnanimously.

And theeere it was. Tick tittered, and I elbowed them.

Grisha raised his finger, oblivious. "Ah! My gift. I've almost forgotten."

He left the room and came back with a box he bought the day before. With a flourish, the dragon opened the lid like he'd expected me to gasp at the silver logo on the top. I had to disappoint him by firmly not recognizing it.

He slid it toward me. I hesitated, expecting some poofy number that had more gems than the neck of a Georgian socialite. Or was it a gem-studded bikini? I wouldn't put it past the horny dragon.

The sapphire fabric inside shimmered. It was smooth, like tiny scales. Liquid and heavier than I expected, it was cool under my touch. I couldn't help a gasp. The dress was ankle length and had it V-neck that plunged luxuriously between the breasts. A sash of silver dangled from the waist, and had tiny sapphires studded along its length. Smiling at my expression, Grisha placed the silver heels that I'd picked next to the dress. They matched perfectly. I noticed a detail I hadn't before—a tiny head of a snake that graced each toe.

"Oh," I breathed.

There wasn't much else to say. Grisha had really outdone himself. I looked up at his face and knew that he knew. Great. Now I would have to admit that I liked something he'd offered me, and that would only inflate the glittery man's ego.

"What do you think?" He asked, rather unnecessarily.

"It's beautiful," I said. There was no point in lying about it. I lifted the sapphire fabric out of the package. It was already pressed and glistened as it fell down to the floor.

After a careful rinse and a nap, I dressed my wounds. The bleeding had stopped at my bicep, but the wound was still visible even under the medical tape. Taking another look at the box, I found a sheer scarf. It wouldn't cover it completely, but it would do. Despite what I had expected, the shoes were comfortable and steady, and the skirt of the dress allowed me the strap of my gun to my thigh. After curling my hair and barely remembering how my mother used to style it when I was a teenager going to a dance, I felt and looked like a Bond girl. I wasn't sure I hated it. When I stepped out of the room, Tick whistled.

"I was gonna wish you luck, but who needs it when you got legs like that?"

Grisha looked at me appreciatively, and this time I let him. Because damn! I looked good. He extended his arm toward me and I clasped his elbow.

"Gorgeous," he said.

"You look good, too," I told him.

"A man is but a frame to the painting that is a woman's beauty."

I swear, the guy just couldn't help himself. We were ready to crash a dragon party.

OMNIA club in Las Vegas had a line stretching out the door. The giant neon letters that read the name of the club flashed overhead as people who were dressed at the top of luxury tried to get in. There was the problem of course, that the milling supernaturals lacked something that I had bled and choked on smoke to get. A black envelope invitation. I have to admit that my breath did hitch a little when the giant troll who manned the front gate sniffed the velvety paper. Had I been wrong and my efforts had been in vain?

I wanted to back away slowly before the universe decided I'd run out of brownie points. Instead, I held my head high as I stepped behind the velvet rope. Grisha's biceps stiffened under my fingers. At least I wasn't the only one half-expecting our brains to mess up the carpet.

The spell prodded us with invisible tendrils. My shoulders slackened when it released me. We were in.

"Two hours," Gory murmured into my ear. "That's how long we have until the Summer Solstice."

I swallowed, nodding. A whole two hours to find a dragoness and an ancient artifact she was hoarding who knows where? Piece of cake.

Holding on to the dragon's elbow, I stepped down the neon-lit hall and followed the crowd inside. We were attracting attention. Even amongst supernaturals, Grisha looked like a million bucks. I did my best not to trip over my heels as I walked beside him.

A glorious chandelier cascaded over the middle of a dance floor. Several floors separated by swirls of light strips that were mounted between levels rose overhead. EDM music thumped over pleasant vocals. Grisha seemed to enjoy the attention a little too much. He kept nodding his head at people's faces. Their expression varied from puzzled to confused, to downright angry.

A few of them looked his way as if they were happy to see him and expecting a little bit of action on their otherwise dull stroll at the fanciest party in town.

"Are they all dragons?" I whispered up at the zmei.

"Most of them, yes," he said.

I swallowed. That was a lot of fire power in one place. My hand grazed the gun strapped to my thigh and I could breathe again.

"How many vaults are under Vegas?" I asked. "This seems like a small territory for everyone to play nice."

Grisha shrugged. "Hundreds." His eyes skimmed the crowd. I had to admit that there was plenty to look at—the dragons and their companions were some of the most beautiful people I'd ever seen. Most of them kept up human appearances, but here and there scales shimmered under the hems of dresses and over starched collars. The wealth on display was staggering and flashy. Some of them looked like they wore more gemstones and gold than could be found in a pirate's treasure chest. Hair was coiffed and shoes were polished. Grisha had been right—had I worn a button-up and jeans to this party, I would've attracted a lot of unwanted attention. As it was, the attention I attracted was mostly curiosity and carnal appreciation.

Gazes slid up and down my figure. The dress had magic of its own—it somehow gave me an illusion of curves. While male eyes lingered on my plunging neckline, the women's eyes were on the shimmering fabric. I shrank under the attention. Being on display wasn't something I was used to.

Grisha grabbed two glasses from a passing tray. This time, I accepted his offer. My stiff fingers needed something to hold on to. The liquid inside the glass was blood red and bubbling. It smelled like cinnamon and rust.

"Chimera blood wine," Grisha said. "A dragon delicacy." He took a long, indulgent drink. "Delicious."

I fought a gagging reflex and touched my lips to the rim. Just another partygoer drinking mythical beast blood, nothing to see here.

A glimmer of gold caught the side of my vision. The smell of real flowers drifted through the chemical perfumes and the blood-tinged wine in my hand. My attention went to a woman seated in one of the private booths. A group of fawning fans surrounded her. Her hair was a cascade that drenched her back in shimmering gold. Her dress was a blush pink and hugged her breathtakingly curvy figure like a second skin. Everything about her screamed virility and beauty. She was the most stunning woman I'd ever seen.

Grisha followed my gaze and his eyes widened.

"That's—"

"I know who she is," I cut him off. Distaste was sour on my tongue. It'd been a long time since I've seen a full-blooded goddess, and her presence made my metaphorical hackles rise. Gods were trouble, and one as ancient as this one was doubly so. "Persephone."

"Her husband is in Hades for the season," Grisha explained. "She spends the summers in the human realm."

As if she'd heard us, the goddess of the Greek Underworld looked my way. Her eyes were luminous and brought Clementia to mind. She'd been just as beautiful, and lit up the room like a torch. Compared to her, Persephone was a conflagration. I tasted peonies on my tongue.

We needed to find the Fern Flower and get out of there.

"What exactly is your plan?" I asked Grisha. Now that we were inside, the possibility of just grabbing a dragon's treasure and disappearing into the night sounded insane. No wonder Tick decided to sit this one out.

"Delphyne's vault is directly under the building," he said.

"Have you been there?" I asked. "Do you know how to access it?"

He shook his head. "That's why I need to find her."

A hysterical little laughter bubbled up my throat. "And what? Ask her very nicely to return our pantheon's most precious artifact out of the goodness of her heart?"

His jaw hardened as his eyes flared green. "I know I can convince her. We have to get to her first."

My eyes narrowed. He was definitely acting shady. In the spring, I had been a fool to trust my boss and I wasn't making the same mistake today. I needed to understand what he wasn't telling me.

"We should split up," I said readily. "We'll cover more ground that way."

His lips moved like he was going to argue and then his eyes glued to something on the far end of the room.

It was my turn to follow his stare, but I couldn't see anything obvious in the drinking crowd.

"I need to find the lady's room," I told him. He broke his stare and looked down at me as if just realizing I was there. "Bathroom?" I added.

"Yes," he said. "Of course, I'll walk you there."

We followed the corridor past the sitting areas and toward the edge of the dance floor. I saw the sign for the ladies and excused myself.

My heels clicked on the tiles as I made a show of leaving. As soon as I turned the corner, I flattened myself against the wall and counted to thirty. Then, I peeked around to where I'd left the zmei. He paced back and forth, then stole a glance toward the bathroom. Running a hand through his hair and over his suit, he straightened his tie. His expression hardened, and he seemed to decide. Turning on his heel, he walked away.

Got you, dragon boy.

I followed him as he ascended the stairs to the stories above. We passed a terrace that overlooked the strip with a view to a row of private rooms beyond. The dimly lit ambiance with the neon light was my best friend. Staying a few people behind, I traced his steps. I stepped behind a couple of men making out, and watched his gaze rake over the platform. He stepped through a door on his left.

I hesitated. Should I follow him right away or hang back? Leaning against the wall, I scanned the crowd and grabbed another drink off a tray. Don't let anyone get too interested in the leggy woman following a ridiculously handsome man to a private room. Just in case someone had been hoping for a ménage à trois. When I'd decided enough time has passed, I saw that I'd been beaten to the punch.

A red-haired woman with a horned tiara glided toward the door. She was wearing a green dress that fell down in a glistening trail. Her petite, elegant figure was all femininity and grace. A slightly too-large, freckled nose and deep-set eyes marked her as not classically beautiful, but her pouty lips gave her face a sensual quality. She pushed the door open and disappeared inside.

"Excuse me," I pushed past the couple that had their masks pushed up their faces so they didn't interfere with their kissing. They gave me a curious glance before going back to their business.

Reaching past the door, I sensed the two souls inside. They were standing next to each other down what was probably a hall. That was good. I didn't need to resort to eavesdropping in a noisy hallway. Pressing my shoulder to the door, I followed Grisha and the red-haired woman.

Inside, lengths of red and purple drapes separated private booths. It didn't take me long to locate the only occupied one. Moving quickly, I settled two booths away.

The drapes hid the faces, but I recognized Grisha's voice.

"You need to give it back, my love," he said. "My pantheon is in trouble because of what we did." We did, huh? Interesting.

"You know I can't," she whispered. Her voice—Delphyne's voice—was raspy and sexy. She sounded like a modern American girl. "We went too far. Now, they won't leave me alone. I can't defeat them."

"I've brought someone who can help," he said. "She is Veles' daughter. They wouldn't dare to go against her."

She erupted in a throaty laughter. "No one can stand against them. Trust me, baby. I've tried." There was a rustling of clothes as she presumably closed the distance between them. "I tried to get back to you."

My palms started to sweat. This was definitely not what Grisha had told me going in. I'd been right to be suspicious, but right now I wished I'd been wrong. Oh, you stupid son of a snake, what had you gotten me into? I considered dropping the sneaking act and confronting them outright. But Grisha had lied to me for days. Who's to say that he wouldn't resort to even more lying? I needed to understand what was really going on. Who was this 'them'? He'd only ever mentioned Delphyne taking the Flower.

"Oh, darling—"

"I saw her, this daughter of Veles," she said sourly. "Beautiful. I almost fried her where she stood."

"You know I only have eyes for you," he said.

A groan rumbled out of Grisha's throat and I heard the mushy sound of kissing. Oh, good, I was stuck firmly in the zmei's personal soap opera. I didn't relish the idea that things could go further than kissing and I would have to listen to dragon sex in order to hear what happened next.

"Wait—" Delphyne's voice hitched. "I think we're not alone."

I smelled smoke. Oh, shit. I was about to become a human torch for two horny dragons. I backed away as the dragoness pushed open the drapes that closed off her and Grisha. Only a few sheets of fabric separated us. I had a couple of options here—try to talk her down and risk more lies, or dragon out and see who had bigger fangs. I didn't love either option. Not only did I not breathe fire, I didn't have wings, so running for the door and jumping down the balcony overlooking the strip wasn't an option. And in close quarters, a well-aimed ball of flame would quickly choose the victor.

"Darling—" Grisha's voice sounded strained.

"Someone is here," her voice turned to fury. "Is it her? Your Vyraj slut?"

Wow. So much for womanly sisterhood.

She raked at the drapes that separated us. Time to smell the fire.

A warm hand closed over my clammy shoulder. I smelled peonies.

"Take a walk with me, Chrys," an unfamiliar voice said into my ear.

I saw a flash of gold, and reality shifted.

11

M<small>Y FEET LEFT THE</small> ground. When the surrounding matter swirled from a golden shimmer back into a solid stone and wood, I stumbled. A now-familiar warm hand caught my fingers until I found my balance. A pair of wide-set eyes beamed at me from a delicate face. Lips the color of pomegranate. Hair like liquid sunlight. I recognized her instantly.

"Persephone."

Something silky was on my tongue. I pulled it out. A pink petal with ragged edges sat between my fingers. The goddess teetered.

"I'm sorry," she said. "Sometimes my essence ends up where it doesn't belong."

I looked at the matriarch of Hades and fought the urge to rub my eyes. She wore the same blush dress and her arms were circled with golden bracelets. Her skin looked like it'd been polished. Her every curve screamed sensual fertility. The cut in her dress crawled all the way up to her hip and revealed a long leg. Typically, I was a red-blooded straight girl. Now, I wasn't so sure. Goddesses seduce and then betray you, I reminded myself. Just ask poor Jeremy.

I glanced around. We were standing somewhere that looked like the OMNIA club. The railings over private booths overlooked the swirling chandelier. Somewhere in the distance, I could hear the techno music, but it sounded watered down, as if we were at the bottom of the pool.

"Where—" I cleared my throat. "Where are we?"

"Behind the scenes," she said. "Don't worry. Your reality isn't very far."

"Are we in your In-Between?" I guessed.

A smile stretched her full lips. "Not quite. We're in someone's In-Between. Trespassing." Her teeth were white and straight as she laughed. "A little sneaking around. Isn't it fun?"

She grabbed my hand and pulled me along. "Look."

Her finger pointed toward the dance floor below. Golden outlines of figures bumped and ground against each other. I recognized the dragons. They were still there, still dancing to the watered-down techno. When I looked around again, I saw that those same golden echoes of partiers. They gossiped and drank as if we weren't really there. Which, I suppose, we weren't.

Persephone grimaced. "Sorry I startled you. You looked like you needed a bit of rescuing."

I regarded the goddess. Being rescued by an ancient being usually wasn't a rescue at all. Running my hands down my dress, I made myself straighten. Countless creatures needed my help, and my partner in literal crime had stabbed me in the back. Whatever games Hades' wife was playing, I didn't have time to play along.

"Thank you," I said, perfectly polite, perfectly boring. "Can you please return me to reality now? There is something important I need to do." Not that I expected her to give a shit about anything a half-human had lined up.

"I know," she said gravely. "You have to save your pantheon." Words froze on my tongue. She smiled. "I remember you, you know. From when you devoured those souls years ago."

"I—"

"You were so devastated," she said. Her mouth softened in something that looked very much like sympathy. Eyes wide, she seemed to gaze all the way to the pit at the bottom of my heart. "You thought you were a monster."

I didn't like this very accurate assessment. She had no business having this glimpse into my soul.

"Yes, well." I swallowed. "I wasn't."

"I know," she said lightly. Her smile was back, dazzling me. "I wanted to thank you. Among the souls you returned, there was someone I deeply treasure. A friend." She cocked her head like a cat. "You know something about losing friends, don't you?"

Not sure what to say, I nodded. This exchange was making me uncomfortable, and it wasn't because of her unsettling perceptiveness. There wasn't the haughty, distant chill of someone out of touch with reality. She seemed, well... normal. Which felt even more dangerous.

"Walk with me, Chrys," she said. My name on her lips was a caress. I don't know what the actual story of her kidnapping was, but this goddess—this woman—was definitely someone a guy could lose his mind over. I swallowed, determined not to fall for her charm. The smell of flowers rose around me as she beckoned toward a fire escape door. Not knowing what else I could possibly do, I followed. Instead of a narrow staircase, we stepped onto a platform in front of a wide flight of steps that wound down like the back of a giant snake. In fact, if I looked long enough, I could swear it slithered.

"The collective consciousness of the dragons created this In-Between," Persephone said. "Only they can walk here. Well," her smile was girlishly wicked. "And me."

"Why?" I asked. "Why are you here?"

She shrugged, the gesture far too human. "This is where I spend my summers. My husband's realm is dark and cold. I miss the sun. And Vegas is one of the places where I feel its touch all the way to my bones. The weeks go by quickly." A tinge of sadness was like a cloud over the bright sky of her face. "Soon, I'll have to descend back into the dark."

"I'm sorry," I said. Even with my distinct dislike of gods, living half your year in Hades sounded rough.

"Why?" she asked, voice genuinely curious. "Sometimes we're called to serve where we're most needed. My soul can belong in more than one place. Wouldn't a demigoddess agree?"

I shook my head. "I belong in Yav. This is where my people are."

"Then why are you here risking your life for your father's creatures?" she asked. I had nothing to say to that, and she pierced me with another one of her bright, dangerous smiles. Her fingers shot out and settled in the crook of my arm. "Come."

We walked down the stairs like two girlfriends at a prom. I felt a hysterical giggle bubble up my throat. Persephone's heels were melodic as they clicked on the granite, and the scent of rose oil joined the peonies. Anywhere else, the perfume would be cloying, but here it smelled like warm summer nights. The surrounding air sparkled and her fingers were silky against my skin. "Where are we going?" I asked.

She didn't answer my question. Instead, she pressed herself closer to me like she wanted to a share a secret.

"Gods are so cold, don't you think?" she asked. We kept going down, and I followed her steps. "We act like this world belongs to us. Like we know what's best. Do you think we know best?"

I looked down at her in surprise. "Do you want an honest answer?"

She pursed her lips. "I believe anything else would be a waste of time."

My mouth stretched into a smile. This wasn't a conversation I'd expected to have with the most famous goddess in the world.

"No," I said. Just saying that one word felt blasphemous, and I imagined smoke rolling out of Stonefield's mouth. My boss would explode if he'd heard me now, and I felt a flash of anger at his indifference over Jeremy. My next words came out in a tumble. "I think gods are out of touch."

Even as we walked at a normal speed, shreds of matter floated up into the air above. The In-Between was moving past us at a neck-breaking speed. I had a weird feeling that we were way past the first floor of the club now. I waited for Persephone to blast me with holy fire, or a tidal wave of flower petals or whatever. She surprised me by chuckling.

"Yes," she said simply. "Most of us are." Her eyes were wide and the small pillows of her mouth opened as her face glowed up at me. "But *you* don't have to be. Your divine can support humans in any way you like, and not only humans. You can make a big difference."

I laughed at that. "You make it sound like I can change the world."

Her smile was candid, like she was about to share a secret. "But isn't that what you humans do?" she asked. "Change things?"

Her hand caught my wrist, fingers gentle. "If you ever want to discuss anything." A string of golden numbers suddenly ran up my forearm. "Call me."

The phone number opened with a Nevada area code. How bizarre.

"Did you just sign up with a cell phone carrier, or do gods have their own network?" I asked, as I looked back at her.

She was gone. So was the In-Between. Suddenly, the space left by her was dark and musty. The scent of peonies lingered like a half-forgotten dream. I was standing in a dank tunnel that stretched in both directions by torch light. In front of me was a door. Without knowing it, I *knew* where Persephone had taken me.

Delphyne's vault.

Somewhere inside, the Fern Flower waited for me.

The lock was a series of dials that looked like someone took a steampunk novel a little too seriously. Codes in symbols I couldn't read were pressed near the numbers that looked carved by Hell itself. The entire system was meant to intimidate whoever had the gall to break in. However, it failed to intimidate the goddess of Hades.

A blooming twig stuck out of the mechanism, and the door was pushed ajar. Something that delicate breaking through modern engineering? I almost laughed at the metaphor. The quirky goddess wasn't anything like I'd imagined.

My dragon's translucent claw pulsed out of my chest. Horns itched in my hair. An untethered soul was somewhere inside the vault. I tasted the stale, cold air coming from the opening and reached for my gun. Something—or someone—else was inside. I could feel not one, but two souls, like a rotten trail of foulness in the air. Not human. Kicking the door in, I swept my gun around. The square space was empty. I guessed it to be around five hundred feet deep. Looking up, I couldn't see the ceiling, but a draft cooled my cheeks. Weren't we several floors underground? I stepped through the space, heels clicking, and desperately wished I was wearing my Docs. The automatic lights sensed my movement and flipped on, one by one, leaving most of the space shaded. I looked at the vaults lining the walls and my gaze went to the middle of the floor.

The Fern Flower was a dim spot of delicate light. Its petals resembled a jagged lily with its glow so faint among the fern leaves it took my eyes a minute to adjust to seeing it properly. The pulse that I sensed had come from it. Grisha had been right. The flower didn't just contain a piece of a soul. It *was* a soul. A pulsing, shimmering soul that had been inexplicably stabilized by being shaped like a flower. My horns burst through my head as my dragon roared inside my brain. I swallowed, my throat dry. It was so beautiful—so vulnerable—that I wanted to rush to it. Everything in my nature told me to shepherd it back to Nav, where it belonged. I took several deep breaths. My eyes swept the room. Even with Persephone's help, this was too easy. What was it that Delphyne had said about someone undefeatable protecting the flower? Just because I couldn't see them didn't mean they weren't there.

"Come out," I said. "I can sense that you're here."

A trickling of laughter erupted through the space. I shivered. They sounded like children.

"Who are you?" I called again.

Two figures flicked into existence. They stood in the shadows beyond the flower, just out of clear view. With small frames and shoulder-length hair, they looked about eight years old. One of them had a face of a porcelain doll—angelic and wide-eyed. A boy, I guessed, from the cut of his face. The other was a girl. Her face was a mask of horror that stared at me from the black pools that were her eyes. Their mouths were a matching set. Sharp teeth replaced children's smiles and there were entirely too many of them. Goosebumps broke over my skin and I swallowed a scream. I kept my feet where they were, but I could tell from their widening smiles that they knew the effect they had on me.

"Prodigal Daughter," the angel-faced twin said. His accent was heavy with Old Slav. I recognized them as creatures of Nav. Dark power rolled off them, telling me they weren't just some ghouls. I was looking at demigods with a lot more miles than myself. "You are finally here to claim your father's prize."

"We thought you'd never come," the horrifying girl chimed. "Seeing how you are too scared to face your own pantheon."

"I'm not scared," I said, feeling foolish. How had this creepy child gotten under my skin so quickly? Really, I felt a sudden wave of anger. "I just want nothing to do with it." Why was I getting defensive? I should've been firing right at them, but their small frames made me hesitate. I wasn't used to shooting things that looked like children. Even though their eyes were far more ancient.

They laughed, the sound disappearing into the air above. I shivered in my dress. A rising tide of emotion filled me. The Fern Flower and these creepy children were making something frustrating rise in my chest. I recognized it as resentment. What was I doing here, trying to fix my father's problems? He was sleeping in the roots of the World Tree, snug as a bug, and here I was breaking into a damn dragon's vault in neck-breaking heels and a dress that wasn't any better than being naked. The domovois had no business coming to me. Fern Flower dying in Yav wasn't my responsibility. I should've just stayed home and taken care of the rescue the ERS assigned me, and everything else be damned, and Zan— Zan.

I'd go to war for you, Veles' daughter.

"Stop it," I said out loud. "Get out of my head."

Another series of laughs, but this time they sounded hoarse and haunted, like they were coming from underground. Like they'd risen from the grave.

"We love humans, don't we, Zavi?" the beautiful boy said. "They're so easy to manipulate."

"And she's no different, Kori," the other one answered. "So full of doubt, so unrooted. Like a dandelion seed drifting toward a fire." The walking horror bit her lip. Blood dripped down to her chin, and she suddenly looked ravenous. "Poof and she's gone. We should just put her out of her misery, don't you think?" Did this creature eat human flesh? Somehow, I didn't have trouble imagining it.

"Don't come any closer," I said. My palms were sweaty on the handle of my gun. "I'll shoot."

"Come closer?" Kori laughed, his mouth opening too wide for the sound. Inside, more teeth jutted out at an impossible angle. How did he close his jaw? "We don't need to go anywhere, Veles' bastard."

I had been so focused on them that I had missed the door opening wide behind me. A screech split the air.

"How daaaaaare you?" A high-pitched woman's scream pierced my ears. "Get out! Get out!"

I whipped around to see Delphyne in the gaping doorway. Her eyes were wide and her cheeks were flushed.

Her face was pure fury.

"You take my man, and then you take my treasure?"

She swelled in size, her lips widening and her body growing scales. Her eyes were two slits that stretched along her enormous, elongated head. The air became charged with the smell of copper. Zavi stood behind Delphyne. I knew what the demigoddess was doing as anger and jealousy crushed over me like a wave. There was no talking the woman out of her fury. Somehow, the creepy Nav twins had manipulated her, turning her into a scaly ball of rage. Unlucky for me, that ball had teeth and possibly breathed fire. I craned my neck to watch as she stretched above me.

Wings spread out through the space, blocking my exit.

Ohhh, shit.

12

D ELPHYNE SCREECHED. HER DRAGON was two stories tall and as round as a barrel on crack. Two wings jutted up and out of her body, and the scales were a shimmering green. I would've admired their luminescence if the fury of her entire being wasn't focused on me. She filled half the space. I had no choice but to back up nearly to the Fern Flower. Whatever was about to go down, I needed to protect the soul. Even if it meant body-blocking it.

"Look," I said, raising my gun in one hand and lifting my palm in a placating gesture in the other. "I have no interest in your guy, okay?" Swallowing, I watched her chest rise and fall in fury. An ember glow swelled between her scales, right where her heart should've been. Was she about to torch her treasures just to get rid of her rival? "I promise that I'll take the Flower and leave."

I could smell her fury now. It rolled out of her mouth in tendrils of smoke. Oh, she didn't seem like the negotiating type.

"You *should* leave," Kori's child voice said into my ear. "I bet she would let you, if you didn't take the Flower." It sounded reasonable, and the parts of me that resented my being there agreed readily. I wasn't cut out for this. Nav's business wasn't mine. My hands rose higher. "Leave, and I'll tell Zavi to stop toying with her. This isn't your fight, after all."

"Shut up," I ground out through my teeth.

Kori teetered. "Another demi bites the dust."

Delphyne's slitted eyes narrowed on me. I'd never faced a dragon head-on and especially one that was so pissed at me. But I couldn't back down. This was my chance to make things right. I was a rescuer, and everything inside me rebelled at the thought of just leaving the Fern Flower there. It was a soul. It was the soul of my pantheon. I might have nothing to do with it, but rescuing souls was my job. The dragon drew a breath full of air. I saw a flicker of flame on its tongue.

Well, this was going to hurt.

"Stop!"

A voice shouted from behind the monster. I risked a glance in its direction and saw Grisha.

He'd pushed his way under his girlfriend's wing. She hissed at him as he stumbled to my side.

The zmei looked like he'd been through a meat grinder. His fancy suit was in tatters and he sported a blooming black eye. He was out of breath as he limped to my side.

"Chrys—" he panted.

His sudden backup didn't make my anger—fanned by the twins and the immediate death threat—go down.

"Oh hi, Grisha," I said. "Care to join the party and you know—" my teeth bared, "explain what the fuck is going on?"

He flinched as if I'd slapped him. "I lied to you."

"No shit."

"Delphyne didn't act on her own—"

The dragoness got tired of us ignoring her. She roared and the walls of the vault shook. I threw a panicked glance up. Was there a ceiling up there and was it about to fall on our heads? The Fern Flower pulsed behind me. I could feel its light dimming. It was like any other soul, I realized. It was dimming away from its Underworld, and right now, it didn't matter if it was a soul of an entire pantheon, or just some down-on-his-luck demon summoner. I had a job to do.

I began pulling off my dress. Grisha's eyes widened as he watched me strip.

"Darling, I appreciate the view, but right now isn't a good time—"

"Shut up," I barked. "Distract her!"

He didn't need to be told twice, which I appreciated.

"My love! My one and only!" he called up to Delphyne until her slitted eyes snapped away from me and to him. "You have me all wrong! I was only trying to get back to you! I wanted to break you out of their hold!"

She burped at that. The gust of air made a fireball soar over Grisha. He ducked it, and continued to pontificate.

"Come away with me! Let's get married in the Ibiza, like we've always wanted!"

Good thing I was too busy kicking off my shoes to roll my eyes. This guy really needed to pick different wedding spots for his 'fiancés.'

"I love you! Let me take you away!" He threw out his arms like he wanted to give the furious, twenty-foot dragon a giant hug. Good luck with that. "We never have to return to Hades or Nav ever again."

My clothes pooled on the ground. I finally wrestled out of the straps that crawled up my calves. I stepped onto the cold floor. My skin prickled. I could feel my horns now and my mind flared in release. Even here, even now, it felt amazing to let my dragon swell inside me. I let the sensation wash over me until it filled me to the brim. Then, I wasn't a human anymore. The release was almost sensual as my limbs stretched into translucent claws and my body lengthened. The room shrank as my view rose eight feet off the ground. Now, I could body block the Fern Flower much more effectively. My tail lashed, and I gave out a mighty roar.

Delphyne and Grisha stared at me. I bared my teeth at the zmei.

Keep her occupied.

Something like desperation flashed across his face. Were the twins messing with his mind, too? In my dragon's eye, I could see his own dragon fighting to get out. Good. I didn't like the way his girlfriend was eyeing this new, unexpected threat. My paws moved back until I reached the Fern Flower. Even if Delphyne torched the place now, at least my body would keep it from going up in flames. Maybe if Grisha could keep her busy with teeth and claws, I could devour the flower and turn back into a human. Then I'd use the chaos to get past them and out into the hallway. I wasn't sure how in the world

I'd get back up to the club without Persephone's help, but I'd burn that bridge when I got to it.

Grisha's hands went up, and he kept yelling romantic nonsense.

If I could throw him a 'what the hell' look, I would. I waited for him to turn into his three-headed badass form. After all, it was the stuff of literal legend. He was the most powerful dragon in Vyraj. I had counted on him to keep his girlfriend occupied as a dragon. Instead, he was doing the equivalent of buying flowers for a bridge troll.

Delphyne looked as over his gushing as I felt. Her eyes snapped at me and her body shifted, drawing back toward the door. She was preparing to attack. This so wasn't good. My dragon body was tough, but it wasn't flame-resistant. I wasn't even sure I had real scales. Laughter rose in my ears.

"The death of a bastard! The death of a bastard!" the twins chanted in my ears. I snapped my maw at them, but of course, they weren't there.

As Delphyne drew in her breath, I realized I didn't have a choice. She'd torch the Flower, and all of those souls and creatures that called Nav their home would go up in flame with it. Whipping around, I opened my maw.

The Fern Flower shimmered as I drew it in. My dragon body served as a container and a protector of the souls, and this one was no different.

Small goat, little goat, come to my stead. The shepherd song that I had learned in my summers in Vyraj lifted out of my chest and filled the air with its silent summon. It was a silly little song, but it spoke the truth in my heart. *Not where, not there, but here instead.* Power stirred in my silver blood, and it drew the soul inside the heart of Nav like a magnet. *I will groom you, I will feed you, tie you to a stake. Come to me, to my stead, not there but here instead.*

Maybe Delphyne didn't have the firepower to kill me. Maybe I could fight my way out. My dragon hummed as the Flower slid down my tongue. Out of all the souls I'd eaten, this one felt like a revelation. It zinged my senses, it—

Made me feel whole.

I shook all over from the sensation. Who was this soul that spoke to my blood like an old friend? The shock of it almost made me forget I was about to become a casualty of Grisha's turbulent love life.

His scream shot through the air. "Watch out!"

I barely dodged the ball of flame that aimed at my middle. It seared my tail, and I had the answer to my previous question. No, I absolutely wasn't flame-resistant. I yipped and fell back, looking for a way out. There wasn't one. Delphyne filled the entire entrance. Her massive body was like a cork that plugged my only means of escape.

Damn it all to hell! If I couldn't go around, I would go through.

I charged, using the semi-dark as a cloak for my partially translucent body. I'm not fully corporeal as a dragon. Instead of a sinewy collection of coils and claws,

I look like a ghost of a wyrm. For the first time, it came in handy as Delphyne's eyes failed to track me. I was about half her size, but it didn't matter when I aimed for her paws. With a flash of coils, I serpentined toward the larger dragon's chubby knee.

My teeth sank into her flesh. I have one hell of a bite. A roar came over my head as Delphyne's maw snapped up in a shock. She screamed fire at the ceiling. My suspicions had been right—there was no ceiling to speak of. Which meant that the shaft went all the way to the surface. That would've been handy if I could just climb on Grisha's back and take a bumpy ride to safety. But the three-headed "legend" refused to turn into his ass-kicking form. Instead, he was running around like a chicken with its head cut off. Flailing his arms, he shot fire at Delphyne. He might as well have swatted a lion. She barely acknowledged him. Shifting back on her massive haunches, she attempted to shake me off. I saw my opening behind her and released her knee. Her giant head came down on me and I did what I'd been hoping not to have to do—use her surprise to squeeze under her body instead of around it. Her ass just barely missed me as I was forced to give up on my half-baked plan. I snapped at her toes. Maybe if I was annoying enough, she'd finally give me the space I needed to spiral between her and the wall. My tail slammed against some vault doors and I heard a metal clank as a few became unhinged. Turning back into a human crossed my mind, but I couldn't risk it. If my attempt was unsuccessful, she'd crush me like a roach under the couch.

My luck ran out. The twins' laughter rang out in my ears and Delphyne gathered her breath. Fire roared in my ears and the air boiled. I was blasted back, my skin blazing with pain. I rose to my paws. Fire blocked my vision. Everywhere around me, the vaults were burning. Damn, this chick really didn't want anyone messing with her 'boyfriend'. I missed Jennie and the heel she'd used as a weapon.

The fire rolled over me. Literally over. I looked up to see Grisha crouching over my head with a piece of metal thrust us over both of us. He was covered in flame, but it just seared his expensive suit. I realized he was holding one of the vault doors over his head. The one I'd slammed off the wall with my tail.

"Turn into a human!" he yelled over his shoulder. "I can take us back to Nav!"

Since he was the only thing standing between me and my death, I did it. The dragon retreated under my skin and my feet slapped the now blazing-hot floor. I grabbed him around the waist, naked and vulnerable without my scales.

Fire scorched the air above us as the realities swirled.

13

I wasn't sure if I'd blacked out, but one second, I saw Delphyne's slitted eyes that promised a painful death, and the next thing I saw was Nav's diamond-studded sky, closer than I've ever seen it.

We were flying. So, he could use some of his dragon powers—I supposed his human torch antics at the gas station should've been a giveaway. Still. The wings on his back hardly even looked draconian. They were more like stunted bat wings. If I had a proper diet that subsisted of something other than cardio and Red Bulls, I wasn't even sure he'd have been able to carry me.

When I opened my eyes, we were at our destination. A damn rock in the sky, if Nav had a sky, that is. Air beat our bodies and I could barely see what was below—the ground was a green smear in a black storm that raged beneath us. There was a rumbling in the air that reminded me of cracking stones during an earthquake. I couldn't even imagine what was going on down there. Chaos. Destruction. The kind that made the creatures flee and the land devour itself.

Grisha lowered me down and I was happy that I wasn't wearing my heels since my hands met the ground immediately. My throat was sore from Delphyne's smoke.

The dragon's eyes were wide and he looked at me with something that resembled worship.

"I knew you could do it!" he panted. His weird tattered wings snapped over his head, and fire lit up his hands. "You are truly your father's daughter!"

I retched, loudly, on the rocks beneath.

"Here," Grisha said. Averting his eyes with more chivalry than I expected, he handed me his jacket coat. It was burned at the sleeves, but the silky gray torso was intact and that's the part I cared about. I took it and tried not to feel ridiculous as it reached down to my mid-thigh.

I wiped my mouth with the back of my hand. "What the hell was that? Who were those creepy kids?"

I was about to add a punch or two to his chest for emphasis when dizziness rolled over me. Grisha caught my elbow and steadied me. The whole sickness wasn't the usual inter-pantheon travel kind. This was much, much worse. I doubled over and gagged, since my stomach had little more to give.

"The Flower isn't an ordinary soul," he said. "Your half-human body isn't strong enough to contain its essence. You have to return it. Now."

He didn't have to tell me twice. I already knew that if the Flower bloomed inside my stomach, I would be a goner. My knees shook, and I decided I didn't care about what had really happened in the vault. That was Nav business. Once I returned the Flower, everything would be back to normal. Nav would be stabilized, my father and his creatures safe, and I would be back where I belonged—rescuing idiots from Underworlds.

"How long?" I rasped.

He didn't have to check his watch. "Twenty minutes." He threw my arm over his shoulder. "Come on."

We stumbled along to a black divot in the earth. It was so void of life, I didn't need to ask the dragon to know that this was where the Fern Flower used to be. Barren and charred. I shivered in my borrowed jacket, then shucked it off like a giant carapace.

It took me a minute of shuddering in the gushing wind to call forth my shifter form. She came slowly, scales and claws rolling over me like a rockslide, slow and laborious. My newfound dragon eyesight brought a new sense of emptiness to the space. The absence of life on the floating piece of Nav was just plain wrong. Time to right it.

Your shepherd has brought you home.

I opened my maw, and the light that came out was blinding. Vines thrust out between my teeth as I purged the Fern Flower back to where it belonged. Roots dug into the ground, and the flower gave off a sprinkling of glowing embers that shot into the air above its petals. The fern fronds uncurled and glowed with a green luminescence. I stared at it, in awe. Its beauty was like a stab in the heart. The essence of my pantheon, its very soul. A rush of recognition filled me. The air vibrations stopped and I could hear the grinding of rocks together as the quaking below subsided. The flower was so beautiful, it hurt my heart. I stared at it. It was like all the beauty in the world concentrated into this one object that I had somehow carried in my body. Whose soul could produce beauty such as this? Tears leaked from under my eyelids, and I realized that I had turned back into a human. Grisha slid the jacket back over my shoulders.

"She's..." I tried to find words that would fit, but all of them were too large for my mouth. "A goddess."

There was a long silence as the two of us stared at the Fern Flower. Its presence pumped new life into the pantheon. I could feel the matter above and below mending itself. Wind blew over the valleys below as they turned from yellow to a glistening emerald. Behind me, Grisha drew in a shuddering breath. I turned to him.

His wings went from tatters to a strong, healthy pair that blocked out the sky. His skin was covered in glistening green scales that disappeared into his sleeves. Relief and joy flooded his features. I hadn't noticed the creases of worry marring his handsome face before, but I did when they were gone. He looked ten years younger, but it wasn't just the age. He looked like someone had lit a candle under his skin. Inside his chest, I could feel his soul roar to life.

"You did it!" he grinned as he examined his hands. "I can't believe it, I—"

I drew his jacket closer over me as the realization hit me. "It wasn't that you didn't want to turn into a dragon before. You couldn't do it."

He wasn't listening to me. Laughter bubbled out of his throat and rang up to the sky. He pressed his ringed hands to his face, and I heard a gasp escape him. He looked back up at me, eyes shining, but my attention was drawn to the sky over his head.

"Veles' daughter, you—"

"Look," I said. "The sky."

He looked where I pointed. The diamonds were still dim, and sparse, like someone had pried jewels out of a wedding ring. That wasn't right. With the ground mending, the sky should've come back to life, too. Inexplicable dread squashed the joy in my chest.

"Something is wrong," I said.

A trill of childish giggles rose in my ears as the ground budged under my feet. Two shadows appeared at the edge of the floating rock.

"Too bad, Prodigal Daughter, so sad," they chanted together. "Turns out you're not a true child of Nav, after all. In your blood, yes. But not in your heart."

Grisha screamed. His wings unraveled before my eyes and I saw the jade scales on his hands slough off like dead flakes. As the ground jerked underneath me, I fell to my knees. My skin split and I stared at the two little bastards as they laughed. Stepping toward each other, they held hands.

"We tried to warn you," Zavi said. Her beautiful twin nodded. "You should've left it alone. And now—" They dissolved into mirth. "You will die."

The rock under me shook like it was a toy in the hand of a giant. I crawled on my hands and knees to where I'd left the Flower.

The central blossom erupted into bright-colored sparks. It looked like it was overloading. The fern leaves surrounding it curled back and blackened.

"No!" I reached for it, but a wave of splitting rock yanked me back. "No!"

The blackness spread through the fern shoots and up to the Flower. It crawled up the stem, inch by agonizing inch, before it choked the sparks. I smelled old smoke as the charred blossom drooped like the head of a dead snake.

"Chrys!" Grisha's voice was distant. Shock raking my brain, I turned toward it. He was standing on a piece of stone that was now separated from the portion with the Flower. The portion I was on. His wings were tattered flags at his sides. They looked even worse than when we'd flown here, barely enough to carry him, let alone a passenger. "Jump to me!"

I tried, I really did, for all the good that it would do me. Rocks split the soles of my feet, and my knees bled as I scrambled to him. My arm was on fire, but my fingers still reached toward his hand. I saw his eyes, green and wide, as he grabbed for me.

The floating rock plummeted and Grisha's face disappeared far above.

Moving on instinct, I flattened against the rough surface. I wasn't sure why I bothered—once it hit the ground, I'd be dead. Squashed like a lizard under a stone.

Nav's power, I thought. In my desperation, I searched for it. For a brief moment, I felt it push against me, propelling me upward. I reached for my dragon form, wondering if I could use it to fly. Then Nav's power fizzled out, and I dropped like a rock to the bottom of a well.

My arms and legs flailed. Air thrashed me about like a dog shaking his chew toy. My hair whipped around my head as my hands grabbed at nothing. I couldn't hear the scream that wrenched out of my throat, I was deaf and blind and—

A gust of wind caught me. The open space above had turned into a whirlpool of air. My eyes flew open as a shape appeared next to me.

He was consumed by the wind and smoke circled his figure like a cloak. I saw a glimpse of a bald head on top of a large body that was easily nine feet tall. Smoke, flame and wind twirled where the man's legs were supposed to be. Powerful arms were thrown out to the sides as sweat rolled down his temples. His belly bulged, but instead of making him look ridiculous, it made him look like an ass-whooping Buddha statue. Fire spilled out of his eyes. A jolt of recognition shot through me as I gazed into the eye of the literal storm.

What the actual Hell and all its demons.

The newcomer glowered at me and I realized that Grisha's jacket flapping in the wind was a flasher's daydream. Which, if I thought about it, was truly an HR nightmare. My rescuer twirled his palms in a complicated gesture and I was suspended. Gravity was no longer pulling me down. The djinn drew me toward him and my jacket fell at my sides. In seconds, I was crushed against a giant stomach.

Wind howled in my ears as Director Stonefield lifted us into the air.

14

I HUGGED THE TRASHCAN closer to my chest. My nausea came in waves, and I didn't trust myself enough to set it back on the ground. I was dressed in someone's old ERS t-shirt and leggings that came from lost and found. My back was sunk into Stonefield's ridiculously nice leather couch as I stared at my boss.

"What is it, Green?" he ground out without looking at a projection that hovered over his desk. It showed flashes of Nav; the shaking ground, the overflowing kissel river, and the trees being torn from its roots in one hell of a hurricane. I tore my eyes away from it. It was hard to believe that I had just been there. Now, I was back in the ERS. Safe and sound while my pantheon was being torn to shreds.

"Nothing," I rasped.

The only shock that competed with my mind-boggling fuck up in Nav was my very own boss. I've known the man for years. Now, I had trouble connecting the fearsome creature that had saved me from certain death to the grouchy, corporate-ladder-climbing man I knew and despised. By the time the Heal Hands had processed me, he'd been back to his semi-human form and wearing a stuffy suit that barely closed over his stomach. Really, I wasn't surprised that he'd turned into a djinn. Obviously, I knew he could do that. My trouble was with the rescuing part of the equation. Why in the world did my boss go out of his way to pull me out of Nav?

"You were— Well."

His eyes narrowed at me, as if he dared me to bring it up.

"Yes?" he seethed.

"Thank you," I said finally. "For pulling me out."

He drummed his fingers on the table. "I wish my actions hadn't been necessary, Green. Maybe they wouldn't have been if you didn't do what you always do—disobey my explicit orders."

Our journey was still a blur, and the painkillers didn't help. Henry the Heal Hand had to put a salve on my arm and put bandages on almost all the exposed skin on my body. And it was a lot. I should be crying, I realized. Bawling my eyes out. The fact that I wasn't probably meant that I was in a state of shock.

"How did you find me, sir?" I asked finally. "I thought you didn't know where I went."

"Oh, I'm fully aware," he growled. "If you had answered my calls, I wouldn't have to rescue a rescuer." Smoke rolled out of his mouth. "You are as stubborn as you are foolish."

Well, at least his attitude toward me hadn't changed. If he suddenly went all lovey-dovey, I'd probably have to rethink my entire life.

"I'm sorry," I said, meaning it. "I thought—"

"That I was an oblivious old buffoon? That I couldn't follow your very obvious motivations?" he asked. His eyes narrowed on me and I knew he didn't really want me to answer. "I found you because unlike you, Green, I do answer my phone." My stomach lurched again, and at my miserable expression, my boss set his jaw. "Those creatures that you inexplicably killed at the shrine? You weren't supposed to survive that. Fire elementals talk, and word got out quickly that some black-haired girl with a dangerous amount of moxie had taken out smoke golums." His cheek twitched. "I recognized the description."

"I had help," I admitted. "And from there?"

He sighed an exasperated sigh. "The Brahma shrine elemental recognized those invites that you cleansed and you were seen with Zmei Gorynich in the city. I knew he was up to no good. I saw fire coming out of one of the dragon vaults, and followed a hunch."

I had to admit that I had taken the Director for... Well, not exactly a fool, but something fool-adjacent. I definitely hadn't expected him to trace my steps. This was almost as embarrassing as having your dad come pick you up from the police station.

"I knew that Nav was destabilizing, and as soon as I heard you'd gone on 'vacation', I knew you'd be sticking your nose in that business." At my stunned expression, he added: "Who do you think gave Zan his leave and sent half the demon hunters with him?"

"I—"

"Yes, I know, you're still blaming me for Jeremy," he said.

Whatever I was going to say evaporated from my brain. "Jeremy?" I asked, thinking I hadn't heard him right. I thought I was the only one who remembered that whole sordid business.

"I tried to get him out," he said. Suddenly, he looked tired and ancient. "Did you think that I'd just leave a kid stranded in the labyrinths of Duat?"

"I didn't think—"

He glowered, and I shut up.

"Yes, I never gave you a reason to think otherwise," the djinn said. "But, all these years, I've negotiated on his behalf. I couldn't do anything."

I let this settle over me. "Why didn't you tell me, sir?"

He shrugged. "Because it wouldn't make a difference. I couldn't save him, so I deserved you resenting me."

"But…"

"I also don't care what people think about me," he said. A shadow of a smile pulled his cheeks. "Something we have in common, agent."

His eyes went back to the projection that was showing my pantheon, dismissing the moment as he turned to more pressing matters. I looked at the flickering images.

Nav was coming down like a house of cards. And I had been the catalyst for its destruction.

"When you tried to put the Fern Flower back, it connected to the pantheon, but couldn't root," he said. "I called Uncle Ophis while they were patching you up. He confirmed my suspicions."

I clutched the trashcan at the memory of the Fern Flower spreading out in my body. It had been so close to blooming that it almost tore me apart and it still hadn't been enough.

"What about Zan?" I asked.

His face darkened. "I've lost contact with the Hrom brothers since we got back."

My stomach turned over, and I could barely hold on to the water Henry had made me drink.

There was a knock on the door, and a pinch-faced Seline poked her head in. The undine looked even greener than usual.

"There's someone here to see Chrys, sir," she said. "I told him you were busy, but he—"

A commotion echoed down the hall behind her. I recognized the voice immediately, and anger boiled inside me. Setting the bucket down, I stumbled to the door and glared down the hall.

"Let me through!" the man howled. He looked like he'd been running from hell hounds in an Armani suit with a missing jacket. Curly hair tangled around his face, green eyes wild, he looked like a millionaire on drugs. He caught the sight of me and his relief was so palpable he sank against a desk. "Darling! You're alive!"

I leaned against the door frame and crossed my arms over my chest. A pang shot through my stomach when I straightened, but there was no way I was going to face this asshole stooped over.

"Oh, look, it's my very honest friend, Zmei Gorynich." I gave him my best withering glare. "Did you come to tell me more lies that will get me killed? The last round didn't quite finish the job."

"I didn't—" he swatted at a burly werewolf accountant who gripped his shoulder. It did absolutely nothing to the paper pusher. I gave the werewolf an "it's okay" look, and the zmei stumbled forward from his grasp and toward me. "I'm sorry—"

Heat blazed against my back. I didn't have a chance to react as Stonefield pushed past me and toward Grisha. His body smoked through his suit and the wind picked up papers off the surrounding desks. Shooting out, his hand grabbed the zmei by the neck and slammed him down onto a table.

"I don't care who the fuck you think you are," my boss roared into his face. Flame shot out of his mouth and would've scorched Grisha's eyebrows if the dragon wasn't flame-resistant. "You will never put one of my own in danger again, you got it?"

"I was— trying to help!" the dragon gasped.

Whoa. Licking my lips, I stepped toward them. "It's okay, Director," I managed.

In a moment that I'm sure seemed like a million years to the dragon, my boss let him go. I glanced up at Stonefield in utter shock. He had actually defended me against an ancient creature. Damn. I wasn't sure if I should be relieved or terrified to have Stonefield in my corner.

Grisha rose from the desk. Glaring at Stonefield, he brushed off his shirt like it wasn't already hanging by a literal thread.

"I brought your things," he said to me. The pleading was back in his voice. "From the hotel."

"Actually," a voice said into my ear. "That was my idea."

If I didn't feel like death had warmed over me, I would've started. A wide grin was the first thing I saw as the person suddenly standing next to me shed off the camouflage spell. The sight of bright orange hair, and the glimmer of the mage hand made my mouth quirk.

"Of course, it was," I said to Tick. They had my scuffed duffel bag hanging from their shoulder. "I never thought I'd see you set foot into the Spiral building. Without handcuffs that is."

Their upper lip curled. "I won't make it a habit."

I looked back at Grisha.

"Why didn't you just tell me the truth?" I asked him. I was so, so tired. My bones ached as if I'd done two weeks of rescues without sleep. "For example, about your girlfriend being mind-controlled by a pair of creepy twins?"

"I—" His shoulders sank, and I almost felt sorry for him. Almost. "I didn't have a choice. We were running out of time."

My boss scowled at the office staff gawking at this distraction in their daily tedium. One thin-lipped vodyanoi dipped his donut into his coffee cup as his enormous eyes stared at Handy.

"Into the office!" Stonefield bellowed at us. "The entire circus of you!"

I wanted to tell him that he was the one who was escalating the situation, but I valued my life.

Inside the office, he slammed the door shut. Then he stabbed a sausage finger into Grisha's chest.

"You," he snarled. "Explain or I'll tear your head off."

Now that was a top ERS negotiating technique. I crossed my arms over my chest and raised my eyebrows at the dragon. Tick snickered and my boss glared at them.

"Shut up before I start asking who the hell *you* are." The trickster raised their hands in supplication.

"Start with the twins," I said to Grisha. "They're at the top of the list of things I should've known before agreeing to break into another's dragon's vault, *darling*."

"Chrys—" he started.

"Or," I thrust my thumb at Stonefield. "He'll tear your head off." Something like a smile tugged the corner of my boss' mouth.

Grisha sighed and dropped into a chair. His elbows rested on his knees.

"Kori and Zavi," he said, voice hollow. "They are children of Likho the One-Eyed, and they're lords of Nav."

I frowned, trying to remember what I'd learned years ago while visiting my father.

"I thought the demigods of Nav mostly stayed in the human world." I cocked my head. "Starting wars and whatnot."

The dragon nodded. "And they do. Kori and Zavi are greed and jealousy personified. Las Vegas is their favorite playground. Typically, they don't visit your father's Underworld for decades. That changed last month."

My boss didn't answer, and Grisha continued. "I made a deal with the twins."

Even I knew that hadn't been a good idea. Something about those two made my skin crawl.

"You promised them the Flower," I guessed.

He winced, then nodded.

"And in exchange, they promised me a permanent place in Yav. A legal place that wouldn't send the Spiral after me, and I'd get to keep my riches." He threw Stonefield a look that bordered on resentment. "Your organization doesn't make living on the fringes easy. I wanted to believe them, so I did. I know," he added at my incredulous look. "It's hard to imagine me being such a fool."

"Well," Tick drawled, "not *that* hard."

"The twins thrive on corruption. They can't act on their own without a host to manipulate." The next part came harder to him. "They used Delphyne to take the Flower from me. When I realized what they'd done, I tried to bring her back, but—"

The way his voice hitched made me think that something else was at stake. Something that was more important to the zmei than his girlfriend or his pantheon or his treasures. His inability to turn into a dragon in the vault came back to me. He'd been desperate, impotent. Scared.

"They took your shifter form, didn't they?" I said.

He laughed, the sound hoarse. "They didn't have to take it. Without the Fern Flower powering the pantheon, Nav's creatures are diminished. Now, I am just a shell of a dragon, a broken husk."

I wanted to bite his head off for being so selfish and stupid, for putting everyone in the pantheon at risk. His actions were already having catastrophic effects, and I wasn't sure how many of them would leave permanent damage. I couldn't bring myself to get angry. Half my life, I thought my dragon was a monster, but she was still mine. To lose her, lose that part of myself, would've been... I shuddered. Zmei Gorynich was born a dragon. His human form was his second skin, not his first. He was a son of Nav and his powers were born from its rich, magical soil. If there was any fairness in the universe, the zmei had already faced karma.

He wasn't the only broken one. After I'd tasted the Flower, its absence was like a missing organ. Knowing that it was dead and Zan was missing made me slump against Stonefield's table. Vyraj's time was running out as quickly as the sand from the hundred hourglasses in the djinn's office.

15

After Stonefield left the office to scream into his cellphone, Tick looked around shrewdly.

"Does the fat man have snacks in here?" they asked.

I shook my head. "The cafeteria is on the floor below us. Need some cash?" They scoffed and Handy wiggled its fingers. I couldn't help a small smile. "Five finger discount, got it."

The trickster and his partner in crime literally disappeared through the door. I leaned against the table and rubbed the bridge of my nose. I couldn't look at Grisha, who was currently staring at the floor.

"Are they going to arrest me?" he asked. He sounded a little too hopeful, and I wasn't in the mood to deal with his melodrama.

"I don't know," I said. "Maybe we can share a cell."

He looked up, surprised. "This wasn't your fault."

I laughed, and the sound was bitter in my ears. "Like hell it wasn't. I ruined it all, didn't I? Some child of Nav I am."

"You didn't know—"

My chest rose and fell at the images I still saw in my head—Nav crumbling apart. Vyraj caving in. Zan's team disappearing in the chaos.

"Stonefield was right. I shouldn't have gotten involved," I said. "All I did was speed up the process. Maybe Nav would've decayed without me, given the rescue team enough time to evacuate everyone. Now—" I pressed the back of my hand to my mouth.

I'd go to war for you, Veles' daughter.

He'd dragged me out of Hell. And I had doomed his pantheon and maybe even him.

Turning away from Grisha, I marched into Stonefield's filing room and slammed the door shut. Then I pressed my back against a cabinet door and slid down.

I wanted to cry, but tears didn't come. The entire last week, I had wanted to do what was right. I was going to save everyone, and go back to my life. But what would my life look like now? Without Nav there, and Zan— I wasn't even sure I understood what was going on. How was I supposed to just go home after all that? Bava and her tribe waited for me there. What was I supposed to tell her? That her master was lost because I didn't care enough about Nav?

The door creaked over my head, but I didn't look up. I didn't care who it was.

A flask touched my hand as Grisha sat on the floor next to me. I was too tired and heartsick to glare at him.

"Here," he said, nudging my fingers with the flask. "It's vodka with honey. A Nav specialty."

I was too tired to yell at him, too tired to be angry. So, instead, I took the flask and uncorked it. The smell of beehives filled the small space. I took a sip. The honey spread sugar on my tongue and the liquor warmed my chest. I frowned at the small container.

"This is delicious," I admitted begrudgingly.

"I know," he said with a small smile. "The bees of Nav are the angriest bastards in existence, but the honey they make is magic itself." He drew in a shuddering breath. "I guess I'll never feel their sting again."

I took another bigger, braver pull from the flask. It tasted like liquid sun.

"Do you know why I did it?" he asked. "Why I agreed to give the twins the Flower?"

I shrugged. "Does it matter now?"

His eyebrows drew together. "It matters to me." When I didn't reply, he continued. "Nav became too small. I thought it wasn't enough for me to have trysts in the human world and go home to what I thought was my prison. I wanted to leave my pantheon behind."

I looked at his handsome profile. "Why wouldn't it be enough? You're basically a god down there."

He shrugged. "I became spoiled, I think. Wanted a new challenge in the human world." His smile was bitter. "I don't know if you've noticed, but I'm a capricious man. I wanted for someone to reject me. Someone to challenge me."

I snorted. "You want human girls to reject someone rich and handsome? Prepare to not be surprised."

"Maybe I could've found someone like you," he said. "Someone to put me— what do you American girls call it? In my place."

Shaking my head, I rubbed the bridge of my nose. "You are seriously delusional."

"Because I took my home for granted, my essence is gone. The Fern Flower fueled my dragon form. My home fueled me." He laughed bitterly. "I am no god. I don't make my pantheon. My pantheon makes me."

He took the flask from my hand and drank deeply. I watched him.

"I'm sorry," I said finally. Even with the warmth of the honey vodka, my chest felt hollow. Here I was, drinking in a closet with a hot guy, while Zan was gods knew where. The sweetness turned bitter in my mouth. "It's not a crime to want a new village."

"It is when you burn down *your* village in the process," he said heavily.

He nodded at me and took his leave. When I looked back down, I saw that he'd left me the flask. My fingers curled around it. His home was gone and he would never be a dragon again. It was a cruel fate, but no crueler than for the thousands of other creatures that were being rescued by the Spiral. Even if, by some miracle, we got them all, they would never be whole again. Like Grisha, their pantheon was their bloodline. What would happen to the creatures living in Yav? Would their powers be diminished, their shifter forms gone, their families torn apart? And my father? Maybe Veles would awaken and climb out of the roots of the World Tree. Would he have to start over? Would he be able to even rebuild Nav? Godpower was needed to support a pantheon. Its very earth listened to the blood of its creator. Just like with my shepherd's song, it was the intent that mattered.

I uncorked the flask and let the mouth-watering smell of Nav's honey fill my nostrils. To Grisha, his pantheon was a magical place, even if he'd tired of it. His heart would be forever broken if his golden-speckled weird realm full of magical and dangerous creatures was gone. My whole life, I'd gone thinking that Nav never spoke to me. Maybe, I just never listened.

My phone buzzed in my pocket, and I pulled it out. The images that Rudy sent me had finally downloaded. It was a series of pages out of an encyclopedia in a print so tiny, I had trouble following the text. I recognized it as research he'd promised me.

"*Adamas Erravit*, commonly known as the Diamond Beetle is a variety of guardian spirits most common in the Slavic pantheons. They are most abundant on a variety of humid rock formations where they burrow into the matter and use its minerals to power their diamonds to a brilliant shine, giving them their namesake carapaces. They infuse and strengthen the minerals with their magic whilst supporting the pantheon's natural defenses. In case of a disruption to the elements, the beetle can leave its host and become hostile until it is once again powered by the energy of the pantheon's founding god."

Between the tightly-knit paragraphs, was an anatomical drawing of my golem-fighting buddy.

"In the case of a re-balancing of the elements, the Diamond Beetle will use the magic it had been borrowing from the pantheon to re-infuse it."

I frowned, head spinning. Diamond Beetle that lived on rock formations, feeding on the natural rock formations of the pantheon. Supporting it through magical means...

My jaw dropped as an impossible realization rolled over me.

The diamond 'stars' of Nav weren't just random geological anomalies that made the underside of Vyraj pretty. They were living creatures. And because they needed the power of the pantheon's founding god to function properly, they followed me to the human world. Me. Not Grisha. One saved me from the golems. If they could be convinced to bring the "sky" to its original position—

Grabbing the edge of a filing cabinet, I drew myself up.

"Hey, dragon boy!" I yelled through the door. I was flushed and my hands were shaking, but it didn't stop me from feeling a nudge of hope in my stomach. When Grisha pushed the door back open and gave me a questioning look, I crossed my arms over my chest. "How well do you know Nav's terrain?"

16

"The Fern Flower is a battery," I crossed my ankles under me as I held my cup of coffee. Stonefield was standing near the window that overlooked the busy offices outside. They seemed three worlds away.

"We have to recharge it so I can use it to call the Diamond Beetles at a long enough distance. On my own, I call only channel a few, but with the Flower in full swing, I think I can call them all." At Stonefield's doubting look, I added. "My father is the founding god of the pantheon, his blood should make them come."

My boss leaned his shoulders against the wall. I was surprised it didn't creak under his weight.

"I'm the only one in the agency—besides you and Rudy—with the clearance to enter Nav." His bald head caught light as he tilted his chin. "We'd be diminished. A non-dragon, a ghost wyrm, and one half-djinn is hardly an army."

"What about me?" Tick demanded.

Stonefield gave the demon spawn a slow once over.

"You definitely don't have clearance, and I don't even know what you're doing here."

The tricksters crossed their arms over their chest and Handy made an inappropriate gesture over their shoulder.

"Don't need clearance when I can't be seen," they ground out. "I owe Chrys my life, and I'll be damned if I let her take the fall alone."

"Tick—" I sighed. For once, I had hoped that the trickster's sense of self-preservation would win out over their itching for adventure. Or heroics.

"Oh, come on, this is gonna be crazy." They gave me a puppy dog stare. "Do you want me to have major FOMO?"

I shook my head and answered Stonefield's question.

"That's why we need to use stealth, not guns," I said.

"We need to get past the shit show and to where the Flower had fallen." I nodded my head at Grisha. "He can find it."

The djinn's nostrils flared. "You want to put your trust in this idiot?" His head smoked. "He's already doomed your entire pantheon."

"Yes," I said simply. "He knows the terrain, and he remembers where the Flower had fallen. And," I gave Grisha a small smile, "he has a lot to gain if we succeed."

The dragon inclined his head. "Before I went back to Yav, I saw it fall through the roof of a cave. The entrance points toward the east banks of the Kissel river. I can find it."

Stonefield glowered at me, then at Grisha, then at Tick. If he wanted to be mad at someone, we were giving him plenty of options.

"What about those demigods?" Stonefield growled. "How can you be sure they won't strike again?"

Grisha shook his head. "They got what they wanted—total chaos. The children of Likho want little else. I imagine they're too preoccupied with cheering on the destruction to keep up with our movements. If we're careful, we should be able to move through Nav unnoticed."

"We'll see," I murmured. I really disliked the fact that they just appeared out of nowhere, but then I supposed if they were emotion deities, they didn't operate like the rest of us.

"What about when we find the Flower?" Grisha asked. "It's—" His face looked miserable as he forced the words out of his mouth. "It wilted. Too much of its power leaked into the human world, and we made it bloom at half power."

"It's a soul," I said to him. "But it's the soul of a goddess. I think I know how to bring it back to life."

"How?" Tick said. "We're a bit short on miracles here."

I smiled at them. "By asking another goddess, of course."

Truth was, I had less confidence in the next portion of my plan than the volatile forces of Nav. The beetles were something that I thought I'd figured out. Now, bringing the Flower back to life long enough to activate them was the hole in my plan. Back in Stonefield's filing closet, I stuck out my arm and was relieved to see the golden numbers. They were faint and I had to tilt my hand to the light to read them, but they were legible. Heart hammering, I dialed the number. A few days ago, I would've rather thrown away my badge than ask a goddess for help. But a few days ago, I still had the naive notion that I was helping my pantheon, not helping it fall apart. Desperate times.

It took her so long to answer, I thought my call would go to voice mail. Can you leave a voice mail for a goddess?

"Chrysoberyl," her voice was like a bubbling creek, threating to break into laughter at any moment. "I've wondered if I'd hear from you."

"Hi, uh, Persephone," I said, feeling extremely weird calling an actual damn goddess for a chat. "I wonder if you can help me with something."

I didn't have to see her smile to feel it in my bones. Her pleasure at my request tingled my skin all the way down to my toes. I swear I could smell peonies.

"Of course," she said. "After you brought my friend back, I'd be delighted to return the favor."

I explained what happened with the Fern Flower. The risk I was taking telling another god about the instability in my pantheon wasn't lost on me, but I was out of time, and out of options.

"You know how to make things bloom," I told her. "Can you help me bring it back to life?"

There was a silence on the other end. "You know what it is, don't you?" she finally asked.

A pulse in my chest made me swallow down. I did know. I knew from the moment I had devoured it.

"It's the soul of a goddess," I said.

"Yes," her voice was breathless, like she was talking about something exhilarating. "She was born in Nav, when Veles had found his perch in the Roots and made his home there."

"How do you know all this?" I asked.

"I've been alive for a long, long time," she said. "And Underworlds... talk to each other. The roots whisper and the boughs tell stories." Whatever that meant.

"How do I help her bloom again?"

"She is alive, for now. But she won't be for long." Persephone sighed. "I can give her a spark, but it's you who has to convince her to grow."

My hand burned and yelped, dropping whatever had just materialized in my palm. It was another twig, but this one had golden thorns that pierced my skin.

"Do convince her," Persephone said. "I would hate to see you fail."

17

BLACK SWAM IN MY vision as we passed the gate to my pantheon that was overgrown with golden vines and shining agate, leaving the roots of the World Tree behind. We ended up in pitch black darkness. Only a few "stars" remained to light our way, and their glow was like a dying flashlight in a cavern. I slid out of the van, my boots stomping the ground. Its rumble made my teeth chatter. When my eyes adjusted, I could see light overhead. Slithering through the cracks coming from so far up, it looked like rays of sunlight. In a way, they were just that—sun from a real sky above entered Nav like an unwelcome guest. Vyraj was falling in.

Was there anything left to save?

I shouldered my backpack, the burrito I'd forced myself to eat doing an uncomfortable dance in my stomach after crossing the pantheons. Trying to save the bits of a dying world was a fool's errand, but seeing how I was the one that had sped up its destruction, I was in for some damage control. Also, I realized as I threw the barn doors of the van open, I was too angry at those creepy demigod twins to just let Nav fall apart. They were from here and they used its power like every other creature in the pantheon. Leading it to destruction while my father was out of commission? Now that was a low blow. Where those two creeps were now was definitely something I was curious about.

"Brrr," Tick said next to me. They were dressed in dark colors, and a hood was drawn over their bright carrot hair. Stealth mode activated. "This place gives me the creeps."

I agreed. Usually, Nav was hot and humid with rich earth that threatened to suck in your boot soles. It was a place where things rooted and grew on the fertile ground. Now, it had that indescribable absence in the air. The whiff of a tomb. I grasped the stick that Persephone gave me until it indented my palm. I surveyed the terrain in front of us. The ground was shaking and disintegrating around pathways I might've recognized before. It made them crumble and roll with ankle-breaking pebbles. Rocks fell from the layer above as the pantheon came undone.

"We have to find the Flower," I said. "Let's move."

Grisha and Stonefield joined us as we made our way through the treacherous terrain. My boss looked strangely okay in the ERS uniform. He moved quickly and with purpose for a man so large. Next to him, Grisha looked like a teenager trying to impress his cop dad by going on a ride-along in a police car. I shook my head. As old as they both were, it was amazing to see what they'd chosen to do with their inhumanly long lives. Luckily, I probably wouldn't have to make that choice. It was highly unlikely I'd survive this trip. My favorite tie dye t-shirt was zipped up underneath my black hoodie. If I was going to go out, I wouldn't go out looking like a corporate drone.

Once or twice, I lost my footing and had to tango with the rolling ground to avoid falling on my ass. Leaving a blue shimmer in the air, Handy caught my elbow the next time. Between having to watch the ground for falling rocks and keeping the ground from tripping me, I was starting to feel nauseous again.

"Thanks, buddy," I said to him.

We climbed over what used to be a rolling green hill. It was covered in potholes and the grass beneath my feet was wilting like a plant no one had watered for a week. An abandoned cottage leaned to the side as its roof caved it from a truckload of dirt. My heart wobbled at the sight of it. No doubt Bava's cousins had lived somewhere similar before they had to trust a stranger in a strange land just to stay afloat another day. My foot caught on something and I stooped over to pick what I assumed was a metal object out of the grass. I frowned; it was a Diamond Beetle. Tick stopped at my shoulder and leaned in for a closer look.

"It's one of your bug thingies," they said.

"Yeah," I said. "It must've fallen from the ceiling. Sky," I amended, "whatever."

My suspicion was confirmed—the diamond sky was sparse because its inhabitants had been dislodged and fallen to the ground. Life had gone out of them. I picked it up. It was hefty in my palm. Sticking it into a satchel on my hip, I squared my shoulders and turned to Grisha.

"Where to next?"

He pointed east. "We're starting to get close, just past those groves and to the river."

I nodded. Stonefield panted up next to me. The years at the desk were taking their toll, and I tried to hide a smile.

"This place is a shit show," he said over the rumbling earth. "It's holding on by a thread. We'll be lucky if we don't get buried under the rubble."

"I thought you'd stay with the van, sir," I said honestly. "This doesn't seem like your kind of party."

"And leave you to make me look like an idiot?" he demanded. "Again?" Huffing a breath, he wiped sweat off his glistening forehead. "The debacle with Asmoday was enough."

I grinned. "That is a dangerous amount of moxie, sir."

A fresh tremor of an earthquake made me fight to keep on my feet. Behind me, Grisha swore in old Slav as he fell to one knee. The ground lifted into the air and arranged itself into humanoid forms. I saw something that resembled massive limbs and heads, as if they had been mashed together by a five-year-old. Lumps of dirt shook in their hands and crumbled boulders into the dirt.

In the wilting grass of Nav, three colossal stone giants, their rocky forms towering over the landscape, roared in unison. Their voices echoed through the valley and lifted my hair. I could see tufts of grass on their weapon of choice—they'd torn them right from the ground. Functioning as tendons and joints, roots connected lumps of earth that comprised their bodies.

The earth trembled beneath their colossal footsteps as they advanced toward what they saw as easy prey. Damn, did I wish they were wrong about the "easy" part.

"Shit," Tick yelped. Magic sizzled in the air as they pulled a camouflage spell over themselves like a cloak.

"What are they?" I yelled back to Grisha.

He shook his head before answering. "They're not from Nav."

Stonefield walked up to me and drew his hood back from his shining head. "They're creatures of the World Tree. Harbingers of destruction."

"Are you saying that the World Tree wants to destroy Nav?" I asked.

"Without a functioning heart, this pantheon is a dead limb," he said. Smoke was coming off him in wisps. "Something to prune."

I looked up at the three half-mountains stomping toward us with clear malicious intent.

"More like to deadhead," I said.

A push of air made me stumble back into Grisha. Wind swirled into existence, merging into the form of a powerful djinn. My boss' eyes gleamed with elemental fury as he faced the stone giants. Making us stumble back, he charged the nearest manifestation of the World Tree's housekeeping.

As the first giant heaved a boulder toward the djinn, the air elemental responded with a swift wave of his hand, summoning a cyclone that caught the projectile in its grasp and sent it tumbling away.

My jaw dropped. Damn.

The second giant raised a massive slab of rock overhead, preparing to smash it down on my boss. The djinn was quicker. He twirled his hands in intricate patterns, summoning a gust of wind strong enough to blow down an apartment building. It lifted him effortlessly into the air, just as the stone giant's attack crashed into the ground below. The collision sent a shockwave through the ground. Debris exploded all around us.

Seeing his brothers stumbling like freshmen at a frat party, the third giant bellowed. He unleashed a barrage of smaller rocks in rapid succession. The djinn danced through the air, dodging the projectiles like, well, the wind. He thrust his palms forward and conjured a powerful gust that sent all three giants stumbling backward.

The stone giants regrouped and coordinated their attacks. One hurled a massive rock high into the air, while the others followed suit. The boulders seemed to hang in mid-air for a moment before hurtling toward the djinn from all directions. Grisha and I fell apart as the cracking stones barreled toward us. A chip of earth slammed against my stomach, making me feel like someone had punched in my innards. I moaned, curling around my belly on the ground.

Stonefield summoned a swirling vortex of wind around himself. The stones collided with the barrier of air, causing shockwaves that reverberated through the mountains. The djinn strained against the force of the onslaught, his eyes glowing brighter as he drew upon the elemental forces.

With a mighty roar, my boss released the pent-up energy in a burst of air. A tornado of wind and stone erupted, engulfing the three giants in a chaotic maelstrom. The giants struggled against the tempest, their massive forms pushing forward.

As the dust settled, I could finally uncurl from the fetal position.

Two of the three stone giants had been scattered across the landscape. A burning-hot hand grabbed my shoulder and hauled me up to my feet.

I looked up at Stonefield who was back to wearing his hooded ERS uniform. He could shift into a djinn without losing his clothes. Must be nice.

"Holy shit, sir," I gasped. "I'll never be late turning in my reports again."

His eyes and mouth creased into something dangerously close to a smile.

"If only I believed you."

The last giant stood from the rubble. It looked a little lopsided as the roots that held it together stretched and bent under the now-crumbling rocks of its body.

Grisha stretched out his arms. The flames that burned from his hands were three times weaker than when we'd fought the Diamond Beetles at the gas station.

He stepped toward the last giant.

"I can finish this one off," he growled.

I opened my mouth to tell him not to bother, since he'd probably fall apart slipping on some grass, when my words stilled on my tongue.

The tendrils of light streaming from above were blocked by a mass of rock-shaped bodies. Ground broke as mountains erupted all around us. They broke apart into walking masses of twenty-foot giants that made the ones that Stonefield had taken down look like the runts of the litter.

"Go!" Stonefield shoved me in the general direction of the cave. "I can hold them off!"

"Sir!" I gasped.

"What are you going to do, Green?" he demanded. "Bite their ankles?" He had a point there. "Go bring back the Flower. You're the only one who can. And you," his finger pointed at Grisha. "If you let anything happened to her I'll make more room on my trophy shelves, just for you."

The sound of breaking rock announced the arrival of more newcomers and my heart sank as I saw our opening between them starting to close. Grisha and I had one chance to make it, and it was disappearing fast.

"Where's Tick?" I yelled over the noise.

A shimmer of the mage hands swirled in the distance as something invisible rolled a rock in front of one of the marching giants. The monstrosity sank onto one knee, causing the rock it was carrying to collide with its neighbor. A domino affect followed the smashing of stone bodies as two giants lost footing. Their collapse was accompanied by a triumphant whoop. I saw footprints in the grass as the invisible shape sprinted toward me.

Tick's orange hair flared to life as they materialized next to me.

"I'm staying with Boss," they panted. "This is better than playing bowling."

Stonefield scoffed, but there was approval in his expression.

I whirled on the trickster. "Stick close to the Director," I said, "and don't you dare die!"

"Who, me?" Tick grinned. "I'm too pretty to die."

Grisha pulled my hand, and I looked up at his panicked expression. More giants were rising out of the ground, blocking our means of escape.

"Go." Stonefield's voice was firm. "Go save your pantheon."

Throwing a last worried glance at my boss and the trickster, I broke into a sprint.

18

GRISHA AND I RUSHED into an opening between two giants. Luckily, they were too busy eyeing the real threat—the djinn that had taken down three of their number so far—to care about a pair of fleshy figures twining between their feet.

A massive foot nudged me at the last moment, and Grisha caught me under the armpits, saving me from a graceless fall and skinned elbows. His reedy, tattered wings looked even worse than the last time he carried me. Wincing in pain, he set me down behind the row of giants that marched on my boss like a moss-covered horde.

True to the dragon's word, the cave entrance was nearby. Its yawning mouth looked full of jagged teeth as crystals opened up into a purple-hazed tunnel. I thanked my endless treks through pantheons and my beaten-down boots for letting me run without gasping for breath. Grisha wasn't faring as well—hard to stick to cardio when you're used to solving all your problems by breathing fire on them. The sound of crashing stones chased us into the cave opening and I ran between the crystals and into the glow beyond.

Cool air brushed my cheeks, and I stopped to catch my breath. The sound of battle stayed behind us. For a moment, I felt deaf in the absolute silence. Grisha ran in behind me and his panting assured me that I could still hear just fine.

"How—" he gasped for breath. Stooping over, he pressed his palms to his knees. "How are you so fast?"

I smiled. "For an ancient being, you're sure out of shape."

He bared his teeth and wiped sweat off his forehead.

"You said it yourself," he pointed out. "Ancient."

The surrounding air was musty and humid, as if the destruction outside didn't touch the ancient cavern walls. I could feel the age of the rocks that formed them—they had been here since Nav was created, born of the earth, and my father's intent. My dragon stirred inside me in recognition. We knew this place. I pulled out a flashlight from my belt and flicked it at the rock formation all around. Instead of stalactites that would drip from the top like stone icicles, sharp, clear crystals reflected the light. The purple haze just visible outside had come from them. They framed the opening in an iridescence that would make my crystal-loving mother lose her mind. We followed the descent into its depths.

"It didn't fall too far from here," Grisha said.

The air grew chillier, and I zipped up my hoodie over my tie dye shirt. Our footsteps echoed off the structure.

He'd better be right.

It grew lighter as we ventured deeper into the cave.

"The floating rock," I said to Grisha. "It smashed through the roof of the cave."

He nodded. "It should be ahead."

I didn't need him to tell me. Even diminished, the Fern Flower pulled me forward like a magnet. My dragon recognized its essence, and I could taste its petals on my tongue. I thrust my hand into my hoodie and my fingers curled gingerly around Perephone's thorny twig. While we walked, I used my inner soul, prodding to feel all around us. Grisha and I were the only ones in the cave.

No sign of the creepy twins.

So far, so good.

Walking steadily, we passed several chambers. Columns rose on all sides, so tall I had to crane my neck to see them disappear into the darkness. The beauty of the place didn't quite quell the pinch of claustrophobic panic in my chest. I prefer wide-open spaces.

We came to a fork.

"Which way?" I asked.

Grisha pointed left. "I saw it fall northeast," he murmured.

I flicked my flashlight at his face. He was pale and his lips were a distinct shade of blue. My eyebrows drew together.

"Are you okay?" I asked.

"I'm fading," he said. "The Fern Flower is dying, and my immortal form is dying along with it." He opened his palm and the flame that flickered on it could barely fry an ant.

"What happens if you turn into a human?" I asked.

His smile was crooked. "You know, I'm not sure. But the years might take me all at once."

Which meant that I would be carrying an empty ERS uniform here soon. I shoved my shoulder under his arm and made him lean on me.

"Come on, then," my voice was forcefully cheerful. "Let's find the Flower and get you fixed up. One foot in front of the other."

I didn't know what I was going to do if Grisha dissolved into dust in my arms. This deep into the caves, I wasn't even sure I could find my way back.

"Hang in there," I murmured to him. He barely nodded his head as it hung from his shoulders. Luckily, he wasn't as heavy as Zan. If I'd had to manhandle the son of Perun, I would have been in real trouble. Where was the thunder demigod, I wondered. How was he faring with the collapse of Vyraj into the bowels of the pantheon? I pushed the thought from my head. We were both children of Vyraj. He had his job to do, and I had mine.

We passed another chamber where the crystals swirled up into an awe-striking flowstone. The light was more obvious here, making the crystals spread rainbows upon the ancient walls. It was coming from a divot ahead. Sunlight, yellow and true, shone on a slab of stone.

Walls shimmered with a myriad of crystalline hues. The Fern Flower was a collection of twisted leaves and wilted petals that contrasted with the surrounding beauty. The cave echoed with a gentle hum, the luminescence of the crystals casting a glow that painted the surroundings in ethereal shades. The hidden sanctuary looked more like a tomb for the heart of Nav. A pang shot through me. Next to me, Grisha moaned. I could feel his supernatural essence dimming inside him.

"Here." I walked him to a stone and sat him down.

"Wait here, big guy."

I took out Persephone's twig and stepped toward the flower.

The thorns, like miniature prisms, caught the ambient light and refracted it across my face and the surrounding cavern walls.

Kneeling before the Fern Flower, I pressed the thorny twig against my palm, allowing the crystals to draw forth small droplets of my blood. Persephone didn't tell me this part. She didn't have to. The Flower recognized my blood as the watered-down version of my father's. The thorns stung more than a regular plant had any right to. It pulled my blood forward, mixing the scarlet liquid with its own golden shimmer. The resulting solution dripped onto the withered, sad petals of my pantheon's heart.

Just like I did when accidentally summoned the Diamond Beetle to my aid, I thought of Nav and its creatures. Not of my duties in the ERS, not of my bed that waited in my apartment, and not of Zan and our complicated history. I was here for Nav. It belonged to me, and I belonged to it. Nav, my father's home. My home, too.

As the first droplets touched the shriveled petals of the Fern Flower, a vibration pulsed through the cave.

The crystals glowed on the walls, flickering in harmony with the magical energy that pulsed from the droplets. Pink and white petals showered onto my head and for a moment, I thought I smelled Persephone's perfume. Then, I realized that it wasn't her scent. The perfume that rose into the air belonged to Nav, and only to Nav. It was warm, like the honey of its angry bees, and rich like hazelnuts. Filling my mouth, it made my head spin and my chest swell.

The crystals embedded in the cave walls brightened, casting beams of colored light that danced across the surfaces. The Fern Flower rose in the radiance, infusing the entire cave with a newfound vitality.

As the Fern Flower unfolded its petals, the air shimmered with the mingling energies and the ground under my feet quivered with a subtle power. As its stem lifted into the air, the ferns surrounding it perked to life. Glowing moss and tiny crystals sprouted from the rocky crevices. My mouth dried. Its beauty filled me to the brim, and words came tumbling from my lips, as if my tongue had known how to say them before I was even born.

"Sing to me, goddess, let your joy of creation fill this earth where I planted you," I said in Old Slav. This time, my tongue rolled over the language without stumbling. They were my father's words, I realized. Centuries old.

"Fill my new world with life."

The Flower bloomed. Its center glowed green, and I recognized the gemstone embedded within.

Chrysoberyl. My namesake.

Swallowing down, I pressed my finger to the stone. It pulled me forward and I yanked my hand back. A sensation of warmth felt so good that it scraped against my caution. I couldn't tear my eyes from the Flower. What had Persephone's twig made me do? I closed my eyes and focused my thoughts. My hand touched a petal and, this time, it seared me with uncomfortable warmth. I flinched, but didn't stop. This next part I winged. Just like my shepherd's song, the intent had to mean more than the words.

"Come to me, guardians of Nav," my Old Slav wasn't great, but I ignored the awkwardness and focused on the meaning, "help me repair what's been broken."

I had no idea if it had worked, but something darkened overhead. I looked up through the hole in the cave, but couldn't see much. Something that resembled a flock of wounded birds broke the light that streamed above and then disappeared. A stab of movement thudded my hip. I looked down at the satchel that housed the beetle I'd picked up. Its pincers cut my hands as it wrestled free. The diamond shone brightly in its carapace and its wings were a metallic clang in my ears. I could barely unzip the satchel fast enough before the beetle burst through. It buzzed like an angry hornet and disappeared overhead. I sank to my knees.

Scraping of feet sounded from behind me, and I saw Grisha rise from where he'd been sitting. He clutched his chest as he supported his frame against the cavern walls.

"I think we did it!" I turned to him. The dragon shook, but his cheeks looked slightly pinker than your average corpse. His frame was racked with such violent tremors that I thought he was going to collapse. Green scales reflected the light of the crystals. "How do you feel?"

His head jerked up, and his eyes looked feverish.

"Ama— Amazing," he managed. He gasped for air as he stood up straighter. "This is incredible."

I grinned, relief filling me. "Feeling better, darling?"

He flashed me an unbelieving smile. His fists curled and uncurled at his sides as if he couldn't believe the strength that streamed through them. Veins pulsed in his arms as he felt his torso.

"Everything where it's supposed to be?"

He nodded, and his face collapsed into an expression of such gratitude that it made my teeth ache.

"Thank you," he said. He raked his hair back from his forehead. Handsome as ever, I decided, but clearly not my type. "I felt like I was lost."

"Oh, he still is," a dual voice that wasn't a voice crawled into my ears. It came from nowhere and everywhere at once. "He doesn't exactly belong to himself. Not anymore."

I swayed back on my haunches and tried to body block the Fern Flower as Grisha's eyes widened in panic.

"No!" he gasped. His fingers dug into his hair as he screamed curses in Old Slav. "You can't take me again!"

"Oh, you foolish dragon." Manic giggles broke over my skin. "We never went anywhere." I looked in horror as two small shadows stepped out of the zmei. "We were with you the whole time."

This was impossible. I'd never felt their presence as we entered the pantheons. What were they doing here?

Kori and Zavi are greed and jealousy personified. They can't act on their own without a host to manipulate.

That's what Grisha had said back in Stonefield's office. Emotions lived in the heart, and boy, oh, boy did the zmei have plenty of both emotions to play with. That allowed the demigods to piggy-back a ride inside Grisha, I realized. I didn't sense another soul except for the dragon's—and how could I? They simply used his. Just like they'd used Delphyne's.

A guttural growl echoed through the cavern, sending a spike of horror down my spine. Before I could react, the twin shadows merged together and jumped into Grisha's cowering frame.

His eyes looked back at me, sane for one last terrible moment. "Run!"

Form twisting, his eyes blazed with green fire as madness took him. The air cracked with malevolence as his form contorted and expanded. Grisha's body convulsed, limbs elongating into sinuous scales, and a sickening symphony of bones cracking and flesh tearing filled the air. The cavern seemed to shrink as the monstrous metamorphosis burst toward the ceiling. Emerging from the shadows, Grisha's dragon was as true to legend as my nightmares would probably be. A three-headed dragon coughed flame and stretched its claws, as if checking if they were still sharp. They absolutely were. His scales gleamed with an emerald sheen, and his wings stretched wide, casting ominous shadows across the crystal-lit walls. A red color so dark it looked like old blood flared up his scales and under his chins. His webbed wings stretched up towards the cave's ceiling.

Grisha's once-human eyes now burned with a feral, predatory stare. Each head snarled in my direction.

The dragon lunged forward, heads snapping toward me. His heads were synchronized malevolence. I barely had time to react as I leapt away from the creature. Throwing a panicked glance at the Flower, I realized that I only had one option—to lead him away from my pantheon's heart. My feet thudding against the ancient stone, I ran like a hare from a pack of wolves.

19

CRYSTALS SHATTERED AND SHOT through the air in my wake. Trying to keep to the walls, I ran through the glowing chambers.

The cavern quivered with the ominous resonance of Grisha's roars as I darted through the labyrinthine passages. Shadows flickered on the crystal-laden walls, creating a dance of light and darkness. Amber glow joined the purples and the blues as Grisha's fire entered the color scheme. I might've appreciated the view, if I wasn't seconds from being fried alive. The tall cavern ceiling did little to deter him—his body crashed through lower hanging formations as he followed me. Nowhere for a little mouse to hide.

There was no out-dragoning the legend of Nav. In my human form, I barely rose to his knee. In my shifter form, he was three times my size and had wings to boot. The only thing turning into a dragon would do was make me easier to find.

My heart pounded in my chest as I sprinted through the winding tunnels. A glance over my shoulder revealed Grisha's ferocious heads, each snarling and snapping at the air in search of me. The cavern seemed to conspire against me, its twists and turns disorienting.

I rolled into a nook and pulled in my legs, wincing as I heard him crash closer. No doubt he could smell my sweat and my humanity in his crazed state. Breathing in and out of my nose, I made my breathing slow from panicked gasps to white-knuckled fear. Much better. My gun was still at my side, but I couldn't think for the life of me what a round of iron would do except piss him off. Where were the twins now? I didn't believe that they would just sit inside the crazed zmei. They were watching me, I was sure of it. After all, they'd been spying on me from the second I walked into club OMNI. And this was the second dragon they'd enraged trying to punch my ticket.

"What do you want?" I asked the air. Somewhere near, three heads of a giant dragon crunched through crystals in the alcoves he suspected were hiding me. "What the Hell do you want, Likho's children? Nav is your home, and you are powered by it. Why destroy it?"

The answer that slithered into my ears made me start.

"We want a better home," the beautiful twin—Kori—whispered. So close that I heard every word. "One that was promised to us. All ours."

The other teetered, and I saw a flash of Zavi's face in the corner of my eye. "A new home and a new start. Built on your father's bones."

The first twin laughed. "We'll start with your bones, of course. A good foundation, fertile compost."

I shuddered. They were enjoying the show before the big finale, I realized. And why not? Grisha and I were certainly giving them a good one. It was clear what would happen to the Fern Flower if I were dead. After they exhausted this merry chase, they would make Grisha turn around and scorch it. I wished I could unload my gun into their grinning, creepy faces. Clutching the sleek metal of my weapon, I realized I only had a couple of options.

First of all, I was well and truly lost. Grisha had guided us through the caves, and I had counted on him to lead us out. Getting out by running wasn't really an option. Not that I actually believed that the monstrosity wouldn't chase me all the way to the exit. And catch me. Even if I managed to escape, what of the Flower? Without it, my pantheon would fall. Truly fall. My father would die, and who knows how many creatures would perish with him. Escaping wasn't on the table.

That left me with one choice. And I so didn't like it.

Squeezing my eyes shut, I took a deep, shuddering breath. Then, I left the relative safety of my nook, and headed toward the sound of shattering crystals and belching fire.

"What are you doing?" a child's voice followed me.

"You want to die so soon?"

I flipped a bird in its direction. Pulling off my hoodie, I was left standing in my bright tie dye t-shirt. Perfectly visible in the glowing lights of the cave. I wasn't exactly sure where the Flower was, but knew it was somewhere behind Grisha's thrashing form. Which meant that I needed to collapse the tunnel behind him so he couldn't trace back his steps. So far, he's been careful moving his body through the space. Even out of his mind, his self-preservation was doing its thing. I needed him to get so mad that he stopped caring about it. I grinned, brandishing my weapon. It wasn't just my iron shavings that were good at pissing monsters off. I was a gods-damned world champion.

"Hey, big guy!" I called to the dragon. Jealousy and greed. I could work with that. "No wonder Delphyne dumped your ass, I would too if I saw your ugly mug." Playground insults as a sure way to die? Check.

I let my voice echo through the chamber. "You know what I thought when I first saw you?" My laughter rang out. "Now there's a guy who couldn't hold a candle to the human men. I bet all your conquests ran back to their boyfriends as soon as they got in your pants."

The three-throated roar vibrated the ceiling of the cave, and massive claws stomped in my direction. That's right, I thought, come to mama.

"Is that why you like being rich?" I yelled over the noise. "Compensating for something?"

With the sound of crashing rocks, Grisha's massive body tunneled through to me like a murderous sand worm.

"Stop!" Kori's angelic face flashed in my vision.

"You're ruining the fun!"

I laughed, loud and obnoxious, as Grisha's three pairs of eyes glared down at me. His giant chest expanded with a flickering fire in its midst. He reared up on his hind legs and his wings scraped the top of the cave. They dislodged the stones that hung overhead and showered them onto the ground. Good.

I narrowed my eyes, as if my heart wasn't thumping away, and I'd just become miraculously fireproof. My head filled with a high-pitched noise that pointed to my adrenaline maxing the shit out.

"Delphyne never loved you," I said, punctuating every word, and went for the jugular. "She just used you for your gold."

Grisha exploded up into the ceiling of the cave. Fire burst up and coated the stone. This was my cue.

I turned on my heel and ran.

If you've never run from a fire-breathing, three-headed dragon through ankle-breaking terrain, I don't recommend it. The colors of my t-shirt kept the target on my back nice and bright. Sweat rolling into my eyes, I led him toward the chambers with the lowest ceilings. Each stone that collapsed in his wake was music to my ears, not that I had time to enjoy it, given my impending doom and all. Whipping around, I caught sight of his blazing green eyes. His maws were so huge, I didn't really have to aim. Iron pellets flew into his mouth, his lolling tongues, and his necks. It had the desire affect.

Wings exploding out of his body, Grisha burst toward the ceiling. I kept going. The more rockfall between him and the Fern Flower, the better. Good luck using him to get back to the magical cave, creepy twins. Cave structure crashed behind us as I ran from the fiery death on my heels. Flames burst overhead and I thanked my talents of being a major pain in the ass for his poor aim. He roared, and the sound pushed me forward like Stonefield's gust of wind. I tripped over a jutting crystal and went flying.

Without the long sleeves of my hoodie to protect them, rocks shredded my elbows. I howled in pain. Rolling over, I stared at my death looming over my head. The path to the Fern Flower was blocked. Now, it was only me and my imminent demise.

Grisha's maws looked triumphant at my downfall. Finally, the pesky rat was good and cornered. It looked like he'd burned through the fuel of his fire, but it didn't mean that he wouldn't stomp me to death. I kicked out of the way of the first claw that tried to crush me. Scrambling up to my feet, my survival instinct shot me away from him. A stone wall met my flight, and my breath hitched in my throat. I hadn't just blocked him in, I'd blocked us both.

Turning around, I saw his heads chuff in delight. The upper most head and his wings made the rock above us crumble as he advanced on me.

"Prodigal Daughter," the rocks echoed around me, repeating the sing-song voices of the twins. "You spoiled our fun. Now you die."

I fell down to my knees and aimed at his belly. No way I could get his maws from where I was standing, and even then, it wouldn't be enough for him to completely decimate the passage. If we were going to die here, I didn't want anyone accessing the Flower under the twins' influence. Then, a very bad, no-good, awful idea flashed through my brain. Gritting my teeth, I aimed between his back paws and at the dark cluster in-between. I'd tried angering Grisha by eluding to his allegedly small package, but I lacked relevant anatomical information.

Did dragons actually have balls? I was about to find out.

I emptied a round of iron shavings in their general direction.

For a moment, the three heads stilled. Green eyes widened at me. And then the jaws howled.

Grisha's entire mass of lizard limbs and mile-long wings bucked up into the ceiling of the cave chamber. The strength of him rocked the floor beneath me. I watched, horrified, as my actions exceeded all expectations.

The dragon burst through the roof of the cave.

A crunch so colossal it shook my bones reverberated through the space. Starlight spilled above his heads. I heard stones creak as the structural integrity of the ancient tunnels gave way. As Grisha reared back, an avalanche of boulders crashed over him. I watched as they pummeled his wings and buried the back of his tail. The diamond sky of Nav lit the cave passage, and I saw that my efforts had been more than effective—the walls and roof behind us had collapsed. It would take a movement of the mountains to clear the way to the Fern Flower now. Along with the passage, the stones buried Zmei Gorynich.

He was still breathing, but he didn't have long. The weight of the stones was too great. His eyes still blazed green with madness as he snapped at me, oblivious to his doom. Could he even feel enough pain to try and save himself?

Fresh air rushed in from above and I breathed in a lungful of humid grass. The way was clear. All I had to do was scamper up the stones that covered the dragon's body to get out.

This was wrong, all wrong.

"You can't win without losing, Prodigal Daughter," the twins whispered in my ears. "You might've taken the Flower from us, but he is ours."

Grisha had done his best to right his failings. With me, and with the pantheon. He had made mistakes, but he didn't deserve to die like a bat crushed under a rock. Not when he was so close to becoming whole again. Blood gushed from his wounds as red as any other creature's. Something rose inside me at the sight of it. Wrath and ownership that ran deeper and older than my own bones. Rising to my feet, I shook with fury. Something about seeing the diamond-studded sky back to all its glory made my chest expand. I had made the Diamond Beetles come back and made the Fern Flower bloom. It was like I was seeing it for the first time. My pantheon. Mine. My blood ran through the veins of Nav, just as well as its power ran through mine.

Before, I had used the Spiral's power, then Persephone's power. Now, I let my power course through my core like vodka flowing with Nav's honey. I looked at

Grisha's blood-soaked maws and fury boiled through me. He was my father's vassal. No, he was mine. My soul, my responsibility. Old Slav rolled off my tongue, as clearly as if I've spoken it my whole life.

"I am Chrysoberyl, Daughter of Veles, and you cannot take my subject!" I said to shadows that crowded him. The cave pulsed with answering energy and I tasted honey on my tongue. Nav was mine, and these demigods, these trespassers, wouldn't get in my way.

"I order you, in the name of my father, begone!" I screamed. "I will not let you take him."

I wasn't sure where the words came from, but they burst out of my throat like living things. Under my skin, I felt coils rise. Not giving it a second thought, I shucked off my human clothes and gave myself to my shifter form. My dragon stretched through the tunnel behind me and I bared my teeth at Kori and Zavi.

In my ghost dragon's spectrum, they were perfectly clear. Two stunted figures that resembled human children the same way that a rotting plant resembled a healthy tree. Their figures were twisted and bent like the evil, ancient demis that they were. My human eye saw children, but my dragon knew better. They were polluters. Manipulators.

My growl wasn't human, but it delivered the message just the same. "Leave him, children of Likho. He is mine."

Their shock was almost as palpable as their fear. I let the latter roll on my tongue. Delicious. I couldn't kill jealousy and greed. The universe created them, and they weren't mine to take. But I took utter delight in snapping my jaws in their direction and watching them quiver. Power rose within me, under me, and opened a pathway into the fresh air above. I felt them cower and knew they were at my mercy.

"Leave," I snarled. "Before I change my mind."

The shadows exchanged a quick, cowardly look and disappeared like smoke into the air.

Stones shifted and sank under the colossal pressure of the cave's ceiling. I heard a groan from the pile of rocks. Grisha lay in the rubble, buck naked and covered in wounds. His eyes remained shut, and he didn't hear me approach. Using my paws, I dug him out from under the stones. His naked body sprawled over my back as I pointed my maw upwards.

I didn't think about it. Just like I had done when I'd fallen from the floating rock, I rode the power toward the diamond sky that welcomed me home. My body serpentined through the air like it had been born to it. Which, I guess, it had.

Grisha grasped my neck on an instinct and his mouth pressed to my ear as we rose into the air. Expecting gratitude, my chest swelled as I listened close.

"Veles' daughter," he moaned. "You... I..." He shuddered. "I can't believe you shot me in the dick."

20

The sunlight streamed through the window of my bedroom. I squinted against the light. What is it about waking up at the ass crack of dawn that makes a person angrier than a hornet's nest? I dragged my palm over my face and froze.

It'd been two days since Grisha and I came stumbling out of Nav. The ERS Heal Hands had a hell of a time patching up the three-headed dragon. He was lucky to be alive, sore genitals and all. My wounds had been more superficial, all I needed was an IV infused with healing potions. From the hangover I had later, I'm pretty sure the selkies put some pixie dust into the drip. While Grisha was in recovery, they had sent me home while the rest of the ERS extracted the demon hunters from Nav. Alone.

The problem was that I wasn't alone anymore. I could sense another person's soul in my room, and they weren't supposed to get past my wards. I grabbed my gun and pointed it at the man sitting in the armchair in front of my bed.

"Hey," a familiar voice said over my head. He was smiling, and it reached all the way down to my bones. "Sorry to just drop in."

Not believing my eyes, I looked at Zan.

"You really should stop pointing your gun at me, people will talk," he said.

"Zan," I breathed. Setting the weapon aside, I stumbled off the bed and toward him. He met me halfway and crushed me against his chest. He felt solid, which was good. I was afraid that this was another one of my dreams. Breathing in the scent of rain mixed with citrusy leather, I let myself bask in his warmth. Then, my eyes flew open. I pushed away from him.

I cleared my throat. "You're in one piece," I said.

He smiled. "So are you."

A silence stretched between us. We hadn't seen each other since he'd appeared on my balcony and asked me for help. So much had happened since.

My eyebrows drew together. "How did you get in?"

He nodded his head toward the living room. "Bava let me in."

"Oh, right," I had nearly forgotten about the domovois. "Of course."

This was awkward. I didn't have a clue what to say to Zan when we weren't fighting. So, I was only too happy to be distracted by the smell of pancakes wafting from the kitchen. I glanced up at the thunder demigod.

"Did you make me breakfast?" I asked.

He shrugged. "I had a little help."

In the kitchen, I realized that he'd had more than just a little help. In fact, I barely recognized my own home.

The floor was clear of all laundry, dirty and otherwise. Not a single sock was in sight, and the carpet smelled like soap. The windows gleamed, and the curtains were whiter than I ever remembered them being. The kitchen counters shone with polish and someone had even gone to the trouble of wiping dust off the cabinets. Instead of leftover takeout, there was a stack of pancakes and maple syrup on my tiny kitchen table.

Zan grinned at my expression.

"Bava and her cousins took some liberties," he said. "Sit."

Shell-shocked, I slid into a chair opposite him.

My mouth watered at the food in front of me, but my eyes went to the son of Perun.

"Not that I'm not happy to see you," I started. I skipped over the fact that I was more than just happy to see him—I felt like butter melting in the sun from him just sitting there. He dwarfed my apartment with his frame, but I was digging the crowding. "But why are you here? Is Vyraj okay?"

"Yes," he said. "Thanks to our joint efforts, the damage has stopped, and the repairs can begin." I was relieved to hear it, but his voice didn't sound as pleased as it should've been. "Bava's family will be home soon."

"But?" I prompted.

"But, it's time to tell you what I was doing while I was gone," he said. I stiffened at his tone, my arms crossing over my chest. From his voice, I wasn't going to like what came next. "My father was furious I saved you, yes, but it wasn't just that. The damage to the roots of the World Tree in front of the Gates of Hell raised his suspicions. And mine." He folded his tattooed fingers in front of him. I nodded, thinking of Uncle Ophis and his inspection of the roots.

"They're going to recover, aren't they?" I asked. "The World Tree powers the universe. It's beyond corruption. The way he looked at me made nervous. "Isn't it?"

He didn't reply. "This morning, I went to the gates of Nav."

I shook my head, hating that I knew what he was about to say. "This can't be right, Uncle Ophis—"

"Confirmed my suspicions," he finished for me. "The roots that lead up to Nav are corrupted with the same magic that plagues the Gates of Hell. No ERS van can drive over them without falling through."

I frowned. "Are you saying that something is destabilizing the Underworlds in order to corrupt the roots?"

Zan shook his head. "Not something. Someone. And this someone has hit several smaller Underworlds already, too." His fists curled on the table.

I didn't want to hear his next words.

"The roots of the World Tree are dying," he said. "And someone is killing them."

THE END

About the Author

Elena Sobol is many things, but she's definitely—definitely—not five pigeons wearing a trench coat. She lives in Utah with her husband, son, and a very spoiled cat.

To keep up with her shenanigans, visit:
www.elenasobolauthor.com

Or use the QR code below to sign up for her newsletter to receive updates on new books, art, and life.

Printed in Great Britain
by Amazon